It was bliss.
Sheer, sweet heaven.

The party went on around them but neither was aware of it, and when Alejandro's mouth left hers to burn a trail down the arch of her throat, Tanya could not stop him. It was a mutual hungering of like souls; it was the sweetest torture imaginable, setting her body on fire, pulses pounding, desire coursing through each and every one of her veins.

Born in the industrial heart of England, **MARGARET MAYO** now lives with her husband in a pretty Staffordshire canal-side village. Once a secretary, she turned her hand to writing her books both at home and in exotic locations, combining her hobby of photography with her research.

MARGARET MAYO

Bitter Memories

Harlequin Books

TORONTO • NEW YORK • LONDON
AMSTERDAM • PARIS • SYDNEY • HAMBURG
STOCKHOLM • ATHENS • TOKYO • MILAN
MADRID • WARSAW • BUDAPEST • AUCKLAND

ISBN 0-373-18660-6

BITTER MEMORIES

First North American Publication 1997.

CHAPTER ONE

TANYA could not believe her bad luck. The reason she had consistently put off visiting her sister in Tenerife was because she was afraid of bumping into Alejandro. And now, almost before she had set foot on foreign soil, he was here at the airport, instantly recognisable, instantly causing her heart to quicken its beats, instantly causing confusion in her mind.

He was as devastatingly handsome as she remembered, taller than most of his compatriots, his shiny black hair cut well above the collarline, his eyes—those soul-searching brown eyes which had frequently reduced her to jelly—enviably large and thickly fringed, his lips full and sensual. She would have lied had she said she did not feel anything, but her pain over the way they had parted, and the subsequent news that had filtered through to her that he was married, was a much more dominant emotion.

'Tanya! Tanya! Over here.'

Her sister's excited voice reached Tanya above the noise and general confusion of exiting passengers. She was not the only one to hear it. Alejandro turned his head and looked in Charlene's direction, and then from her to Tanya. It all happened in a split second; their eyes met and she saw the sudden narrowing in his before his attention was taken up by the beautiful woman who threw herself into his arms, a woman with jet-black hair piled on top of her head, perfectly applied make-up, elegantly dressed. Tanya's bitterness deepened. She had wondered what his wife looked like. Now she knew. And she would have given anything to be able to turn right round and catch the same plane back to England.

7

By this time Charlene had pushed her way to Tanya's side and was welcoming her sister enthusiastically. When Tanya next looked in Alejandro's direction he had gone. Maybe she had even imagined him? Although she knew she hadn't. It was all wishful thinking. She ought to have followed her instincts and never let Charlene persuade her to come here. The holiday was going to be a disaster. The next instant a card was being pushed into her hand and a well-remembered voice growled low in her ear, 'I would like to talk with you. Give me a ring.'

He disappeared as quickly as he had approached. Charlene looked at her sister in amazement. 'Was that who I thought it was?'

Tanya nodded. 'The very same.'

'I cannot believe it. In the two years I've been out here I've never seen him, not once.'

'I know, you told me,' muttered Tanya unhappily. 'It was what finally persuaded me to come. Hell, I wish I hadn't; he's going to ruin my holiday.'

'Rubbish, you won't see him again.' Charlene's tone was positive, her arm protectively around her younger sister. 'What did he want anyway?'

'He said he wanted to talk to me.'

'What a nerve.' Charlene was incensed. 'Is this his address?' She plucked the card from Tanya's hand and tore it into pieces, throwing them into the air where they fell like confetti.

Charlene was the elder of the two sisters, taller and heavier, and had always had more to say for herself. Not that Tanya was lacking in confidence; far from it. Having lost both their parents at a very tender age, they had been brought up separately by a succession of foster-parents, some not always happy experiences, and they had frequently needed to stand up for themselves.

Tanya's shoulder-length hair was a soft honey-gold, in complete contrast to Charlene's raven darkness. The only things they had in common were their eyes, sloe-shaped and a beautiful azure-blue.

'Come along.' Charlene picked up Tanya's case. 'My car's in the car park. Let's forget we ever saw that man; he's bad news without a doubt.'

Tanya followed her sister through the line of people waiting for taxis and over the road to the busy car park. The warmth of the day after England's freezing winter temperatures was blissful, and she shrugged off her jacket as she walked. Seeing Alejandro at the airport had put a damper on her spirits, but she was determined not to let it get her down. Charlene was probably right; they wouldn't see him again.

'Here we are.' Her sister's voice cut into her thoughts. She opened the boot of a smart white car and threw Tanya's case inside. 'Let's go.'

Alejandro was forgotten as they left the airport and hit the motorway. Tanya gazed with interest at her surroundings; the bare, jagged mountains in the distance, their tops draped in mist; the brown, barren countryside with just the odd shrub or clump of prickly pear growing tenaciously in the dry earth; the occasional flush of buildings, some industrial, some purpose-built holiday developments close to the shore.

It was all new and exciting, and she did not want to miss a thing. Charlene had recently moved in with a family whose daughter worked in the same hotel as Charlene, and they had become good friends. The girl's mother had agreed to Tanya's spending her holiday with them as well. Tanya found it difficult to believe the woman's generosity to a complete stranger.

They soon left the motorway and headed up into the hills, the road curving and climbing, bushes of white daisy-like flowers and clumps of spiny cactus adorning the roadside. They passed through a dusty village where old men sat outside bars and children kicked balls or rode BMXs, and passed several isolated houses on the outskirts; square, box-like dwellings built out of blocks. Some had been whitewashed, some were still bare concrete, looking, to Tanya's English eyes, as though they were not finished. One or two had pantiled roofs and looked more attractive, but when Charlene turned off the road and pulled up beside one of the unpainted buildings Tanya looked at her with a frown. 'Is this where you're living?'

Charlene smiled and nodded. 'It's not like it looks, I assure you. It's heavenly inside; most of them are. You can't go by external appearances. I was once told that it was because the Canarians didn't care what a house looked like on the outside, as we do — but I later learned that the real reason is that they don't have to pay taxes on unfinished buildings. The government run campaigns sometimes to try to get people to paint their walls white, but they're always a failure.'

Still looking doubtful, Tanya followed her sister. The single-storey building was an odd shape, as though it had had further rooms built on as and when the need arose. There was a wall, built yet again out of grey blocks, denoting the boundary of the property, but there was no garden as such, just a few straggly plants growing and a dog foraging. Coming from her smart semi-detached house on the outskirts of Sheffield, with its tidy green and abundant garden, Tanya found it difficult to feel happy about spending a month here.

All the windows were shuttered — wooden, varnished shutters — and the front door was wooden too. In fact it was an ornately carved, expensive-looking door which looked oddly out of place with its surroundings. And once inside Tanya could see what Charlene meant. The cool, clean hallway boasted a tiled floor, a polished chair in the corner and a profusion of healthy plants which hung and sat and filled every corner. It was like an oasis in the desert.

In the shadowy living-room Charlene's friend's mother waited to greet her. The tiny woman was dressed all in black, her greying hair secured in a neat

bun. She smiled warmly as Charlene made the introductions in fluent Spanish and held out her hand. Tanya
smiled back. 'It's very kind of you to let me stay here.'
she said.

Through her sister she established that Señora
Guerra was very pleased to welcome her into their
house and she was to treat it as her home and come
and go as she pleased and not to worry about disturbing
them.

Tanya was grateful her sister spoke the language—it
had actually been a prerequisite of her job at the hotel.
In fact Charlene spoke several languages. Tanya, on
the other hand, spoke no more than schoolgirl French.

'She's a wonderful lady,' Charlene told her. 'Señor
Guerra died a few years ago, but she has coped
admirably. Maribel is her only child left at home. She
has three sons, but they are all married now, though
they frequently visit. She's delighted about it. The
house almost bursts at the seams when they all come.'

'I hope I won't be in the way,' said Tanya worriedly.

'Of course not. It was Señora Guerra's idea that you
stay here.' She turned and said something to the older
woman, who instantly smiled, speaking rapidly, gestur-
ing eloquently, reassuring Tanya that she was not
putting them out in the least.

The room they were in amazed Tanya. It was like
going back a hundred years; it was like photographs
she had seen of days gone by. The furniture looked
like oak, big and solid, and the dresser packed with
plates and cups and saucers. There was a settee and
rocking-chairs with hand-embroidered cushions, pieces
of pottery, photographs and pictures on the walls and
more plants standing in big pots on the tiled floor or
hanging from the ceiling. Every inch of space was used.
It was cluttered but beautiful, and Tanya loved it.

She suddenly realised that her host was watching
her, and she gave an apologetic smile. 'I was admiring
your house. It's lovely.'

Charlene translated and the woman beamed, and
then Tanya was taken to her room, which was next to
Charlene's. Again, heavy oak furniture was dominant.
The walls were painted a simple white, only the patch-
work bedcover providing a bright splash of colour.

The first thing she did was open the windows and
push back the shutters, allowing the bright sunlight to
flood the room. The jagged outline of the mountains
was up above them, the earlier mist having completely
disappeared, the sky a clear, intense blue. Tanya was
anxious to explore — so long as she did not bump into
Alejandro! The thought of him being somewhere out
there still festered in the back of her mind.

Her sister helped her unpack, and by the time she
had freshened up and changed into a cotton sundress
Señora Guerra had lunch waiting. A white cloth had
been spread on the table in the living-room, and as
soon as Tanya sat down her meal was set in front of
her — white fish, potatoes cooked in their skins, carrots
and peas.

'Bacalao,' confirmed Charlene with a smile, 'or
codfish to you and me, and these ——' indicating the
potatoes, ' — are papas arrugadas, which, translated
literally, means wrinkled potatoes. They're cooked in
very salty water and allowed to boil dry, leaving a salty
coating on their skins. The Canarians always cook
them this way. I love them.'

Tanya's verdict later was one of approval too. It was
a simple meal, yet filling and tasty, and when she was
offered fresh fruit for dessert she had to refuse. They
drank wine also, a sweet, local wine that was not really
to Tanya's taste, though she was too polite to say so.
Señora Guerra was a marvellous hostess, even with the
language barrier, her actions and expressions when she
was trying to get something across making Tanya laugh
wholeheartedly.

After lunch Charlene took her for a short drive; once
back she met Señora Guerra's daughter, ate another

excellent meal—thinking she would be as fat as a pig when she went home if she went on like this—and now she lay in bed, her head sunk into a soft, sweet-smelling pillow. One way and another it had been quite a day, and she was desperately tired, yet thoughts of Alejandro kept her wide awake.

He had duped her all right. She had never dreamt that he was using her, that it was an affair he was after, a passionate fling before he went back to Tenerife to marry his childhood sweetheart. What a gullible fool she had been. He had even talked about bringing her here, had spoken of the pleasure he would get in showing her his beloved country—and she had believed him! What a silver-tongued swine he was. All the anger she had felt nine years ago came back with a vengeance, boiling, enraging, making her wish desperately and deeply that she had not let Charlene persuade her to come.

And why should he want to talk to her? What was there to say? Nothing! Not a thing. He had hurt her feelings immeasurably; she had given him all of her love, and for what? He was the last person she wanted to talk to now, and she hoped and prayed that she would never see him again.

Inevitably her thoughts went back to their first meeting. She had been eighteen at the time, and they had met at a friend's wedding. He had been working as a waiter in the hotel restaurant in which the reception was held, and there had been an instant mutual attraction. They had not spoken, Alejandro refusing to put his job in jeopardy by chatting to one of the guests, but the suggestion had been there in his eyes that he would like to see her again.

How he had found out where she worked Tanya did not know, but two days later he had been waiting outside the office block when she finished at five. For a few seconds all she could do was stare in amazement.

'Do forgive me,' he said, in heavily accented English,

'but I wanted to see you.' His teeth were white and even, his smile cautious.

'How did you know where to find me?' Her heart began to hammer and her blue eyes were wide as she looked at him. He was dressed in jeans and a black leather jacket with a roll-collared blue sweater beneath. He was fantastically handsome and a whole head taller than herself, which made him over six feet. He was a few years older as well, and she found him tremendously exciting.

'I have seen you many times as I live not far away from here, but I did not have the courage to speak,' he told her honestly. 'Then at the wedding I knew I had to make the effort. I hope you are not offended.'

Tanya shook her head, completely mesmerised by this fascinating stranger. She could not quite make up her mind from which part of the world he came — Spain or Italy, perhaps, judging by his colouring.

He held out his hand. 'My name is Alejandro Vázquez Herrera, and I believe you are Tanya? A beautiful name for a beautiful girl.'

'Tanya Elliott,' she confirmed, putting her slim hand into his, liking the feel of his firm handshake. 'How did you know?'

'By keeping my ears open at the wedding reception,' he confessed with an engaging smile. 'May I take you for a drink?'

'Perhaps a coffee?' she murmured. She felt a sudden shyness which was alien to her, and put it down to the fact that he wasn't English. He was really quite the most exciting person she had met in a long time.

She walked along at his side, aware of the curious glances of her colleagues. There would be plenty of questions tomorrow. 'Are you living in England permanently?' she ventured after they had walked a few yards in silence.

'No,' he said, shaking his head. 'I am here to study English. I am taking classes and doing a job at the same time to help pay for both them and my accommodation.'

'Your English sounds very good to me,' she said, hiding her disappointment that he would one day return to his home country.

'It has improved,' he agreed, lifting his shoulders in a modest gesture. 'I have been here twelve months now. I have enjoyed it very much.'

'How much longer do you plan to stay?' She waited with bated breath for his answer. It would be just her luck if he was planning to go home very shortly.

'I am in no hurry,' he told her.

Tanya's face broke into an involuntary smile of relief. 'Where do you come from?'

'The Canary Islands—Tenerife, to be exact. Have you ever been there?'

Tanya shook her head.

'Then you must; they are beautiful. Politically we belong to Spain, but we prefer to think of ourselves as independent.'

Tanya showed her ignorance. 'I'm not even sure where they are.'

He gave a slow, tolerant smile. 'In the Atlantic Ocean, just off the coast of Africa. The climate is superb. Ask a Canarian what the islands are unique for, and he will say the weather. It is our blessing. It encourages tourism and prospers our economy.'

'So what do you think of England?'

A grimace took the place of his smile. 'What do I think? I am used to it now, but it was so cold when I first came. I wondered how you put up with it. Now I think England is beautiful—not so much as Tenerife, of course, but. . .' He broke off and laughed. 'I am joking. Your country is—how do you say it?—on a par. Each has its own—advantages. Is that right?'

Tanya nodded, laughing also. He was being very diplomatic.

'Shall we take our coffee here?' He halted outside a

tearoom which had a good reputation and was not very busy at this time of day.

Afterwards Tanya had no idea what they talked about. She remembered him saying that his mother was no longer alive, that he had several brothers and sisters, all younger than himself, but apart from that she recalled nothing. She knew only that she had had a wonderful time and that Alejandro was no longer a stranger but a warm, humorous man who had kept her amused and happy and wormed his way just a little into her heart — even in that short space of time.

She could not sleep that night for thinking about him, and could not wait for their next date. He had only one evening free a week, he told her ruefully, but this week he had all day Sunday off and he would very much like to see her then.

Tanya lived in a small bed-sitter on the top floor of a converted Victorian house on the outskirts of Birmingham, found for her by the local council when she became of age and no longer qualified for foster care. Charlene had wanted her to move in to her much bigger and comfortable apartment, but Tanya craved her independence. She wanted to lead her own life.

In the weeks that followed Tanya saw as much of Alejandro as was possible, given that he worked unsociable hours and still took English lessons in his spare time. It was a passionate, intense affair, both feeling as though they had known each other forever, hating the hours they were forced to spend apart, never able to get enough of each other.

When her sister met him she was equally impressed. 'Lucky you,' she said, 'but be careful. Don't forget he'll be going home one day.'

'Yes, but he'll take me with him,' said Tanya confidently. 'He's already spoken about it.'

Charlene looked sceptical. 'Isn't that what they all say? I've lived longer than you, Tan; I know what men are like.'

But Tanya would listen to nothing detrimental about her beloved Alejandro, and for three months the affair raged. She grew more and more confident in her love for him, never actually declaring her feelings — and nor did he — but they both knew that it was there, and as far as Tanya was concerned she was happier than she had ever been in her life.

He showed his love in a dozen different ways; in his caring attitude, in the intense physical pleasure of their lovemaking, in the little gifts he bought her — nothing expensive — a single rose, chocolates, a glossy magazine, bath oils. None cost more than a pound or two, and yet they meant as much to Tanya as if he had bought her diamonds or gold.

Always he came to the flat for her; sometimes they went out, sometimes they stayed in, and once he had taken her back to his room at the hotel. Employees were actually not allowed to have members of the opposite sex in their rooms, but she had said so many times that she wanted to see where he lived, that in the end he had given in.

How many times since had she wished she had never gone there? It was as small and cramped as her own room, but far more untidy, and when she offered to make them a cup of coffee she could not help noticing the letter that had been left lying on the cupboard where the kettle stood.

Her eyes flicked over the boldly written page before she realised what she was doing, and once she had started she could not stop. It was from Alejandro's father, and surprisingly written in English — probably as a concession to his son's improving his knowledge of the language. Although his father's mastery of English was not very good, Tanya managed to make out that he was asking Alejandro when he was coming home, because Juanita was growing impatient. It was time he came back and made arrangements for his wedding, which had been put off long enough.

His wedding! Tanya felt the colour drain out of her face, and without stopping to think she picked up the letter and thrust it under Alejandro's nose. 'What the hell is this all about?'

'You should not have read that, Tanya,' he said quietly.

'But I have,' she cried, 'and I want to know about this girl, this Juanita. Why have you never told me about her? Why have you let me assume that it's me you love? Hell, if I'd known all you were interested in was an affair I ——'

'That is not the case,' he interjected sharply.

'No?' Her eyes widened, full of scepticism. 'It looks very much like that to me. Do you deny that there's another girl in your life?'

'Yes, I do,' he announced strongly.

'So who is Juanita?'

'A lifelong friend, a family friend; we virtually grew up together.'

'*A friend*?' Tanya's tone filled with disbelief. 'It doesn't sound as though she's just a friend to me.'

'Maybe there was more in it once,' he admitted, 'but that was over a long time ago. I have already written and told her about you.'

Tanya shook her head, wanting to believe him, but unable to. If he had written Juanita would surely have told his father, especially if the families were close. 'You're lying,' she whispered. 'You're trying to get out of it. Well, don't bother; it's over. I want nothing more to do with you. You're nothing but a two-timing snake in the grass. Juanita is welcome to you.' She picked up her jacket and headed for the door.

'Tanya, stop!' Alejandro's voice came after her. 'Let me explain; do not walk out on me like this.'

'What is there to explain?' she tossed over her shoulder. 'Everything is as clear as tap water. You've been using me; it's as simple as that. You've wanted a girl to satisfy your basic male urges until you get back to your true love. I feel sorry for her, do you know that? I wonder if she knows what type of man it is she's going to marry.'

'Do you really think I would behave so badly?' His dark eyes were cold, his whole body rigid.

'Yes, I do,' she yelled. 'I not only think it, there's proof in your father's letter. Goodbye, Alejandro.' She slammed the door and marched along the corridor, running down the steps and through the hotel grounds to the street. Not until she was long out of sight of the building did she slow down, but it was not until she reached the refuge of her bed-sitter that she let her tears fall.

Never had she felt so humiliated. She really had thought that she meant something to him. Her sister had been right. If only she had listened, if only she hadn't let herself get so deeply emotionally involved.

For two days Tanya did not leave her flat. Her face was so swollen by crying that she was too embarrassed to go to work, and she didn't even care whether she lost her job. Life was hell all of a sudden.

To begin with she had thought that Alejandro would contact her, that he would come round and explain everything, declare his love, say his father was mistaken, but she heard nothing, and the two days turned into a week, a week of intense misery. When she could stand it no longer she swallowed her pride and marched round to the hotel. It couldn't just end like this; she wouldn't let it. Maybe he had been right and she wrong. Maybe he had written to Juanita. Maybe she ought to give him the benefit of the doubt.

The news that he had gone back to Tenerife paralysed her, the shock of it almost greater than discovering that he had another girl. He had gone without a word, without trying to patch things up between them. It was over, all over, and when her sister announced that she had accepted a job as under-manager in a new, though relatively small hotel in Sheffield, Tanya readily accepted the invitation to go and live with her.

Several months went by, during which time Tanya gradually came back to life, settled down in a new job as a junior secretary with a computer software company, and resolutely pushed Alejandro out of her mind.

Until the day Charlene came home with the news that she had heard Alejandro was married. Tanya's mouth fell open and she felt as though someone had kicked her legs from beneath her. She dropped on to the nearest chair. 'To Juanita?' she managed to whisper.

Charlene nodded. 'I'm so sorry, Tan. But I thought it best you knew. Now you'll be able to get on with your life, accept some of those dates that you keep refusing.'

'But how—how did you find out?' Tanya's blue eyes were wide and troubled, her face pale.

'I got talking to one of the guests who hailed from Tenerife. I happened to mention Alejandro, and strangely enough he knew him—or at least he knew of him.'

Tanya swallowed hard. 'How long ago did he get married?'

Charlene shrugged. 'I don't know; he didn't say.'

So that definitely was the end of it, thought Tanya, as she lay in bed that night. Not even to herself had she admitted that she always hoped he might come back, that he would trace her and declare his love for her. Now there was no chance, none at all. It was definitely the end.

She still found it difficult to believe that he had been so warm and loving towards her when all the time there had been another girl in the background. She really had thought he was genuinely in love with her; she had never dreamt that it was all a game to him.

After this further blow to her pride Tanya decided

that she had stayed in long enough. She would go out on dates, enjoy male company, but she would never, ever, let herself become involved again. She would be like her sister, a dedicated career woman.

All went well until two years later when she met Peter. He was warm and wonderful and kind, and she fell in love. It was nothing like her love for Alejandro; this was a much gentler relationship, with none of the passion and hunger that had so inflamed her body, sent her soaring with the stars and flying with the eagles. But nevertheless she was content, and twelve months later they were married. Three years after that Peter died from a long and serious illness. Tanya was devastated. At the age of twenty-four she had suffered two terrible losses.

It took her time to pull herself together, but she managed it, and when she applied for promotion, and got the job of PA to the managing director of the software company, she put her heart and soul into her work, not minding that John Drake asked her to work long hours, that sometimes she dropped into bed so exhausted that she was sure she wouldn't wake with the alarm the next morning. But always she did, and somehow she survived.

When Charlene announced that she'd been offered a job running a large hotel in Tenerife Tanya could not believe the irony of it. Mention of Alejandro's native country brought painful memories back, and wild horses wouldn't drag her out there with her sister, although Charlene had done her best to persuade her.

'I have my own house now. I'm settled here; I like it,' Tanya insisted.

'And I suppose you're trying to tell me it has nothing to do with Alejandro Vázquez,' taunted Charlene.

'No, I'm not; it has everything to do with him. There's no way I want to meet that man again.'

'You're still hung up over him?' Charlene frowned.

'I thought all that had died when you married Peter. You haven't mentioned him for years.'

'He was my first love,' announced Tanya quietly. 'I'll never forget him.'

CHAPTER TWO

CHARLENE took a few days off work to show Tanya around, and there was far too much to see and enthuse over to worry herself about Alejandro, although she privately wished her sister hadn't torn up his card. Even though she would never, ever get in touch with him she was curious to know where he lived.

Señora Guerra was a dressmaker, with the reputation of being the finest one on the island, and with the start of Tenerife's annual *carnaval* only two weeks away she was busy finishing off the many costumes she had been asked to make. There was a constant stream of visitors to the house, all eagerly trying on and picking up their costumes. One room had been set aside for this purpose, and it was like an Aladdin's cave, filled with richly coloured fabrics, beads, sequins, feathers, each costume taking hours and hours of painstaking work to complete.

Tanya liked dressmaking herself and took a keen interest in all that was going on, and very often Señora Guerra — or Matilde, as she asked to be called — invited Tanya to see the dresses actually being tried on.

When a dark red, open-topped Mercedes pulled up outside one afternoon Tanya thought nothing of it, until she recognised the driver and his companion. Alejandro and his wife! It could not be! And yet it was. She could hardly believe her bad luck. Already she had told Matilde that she would like to see this particular dress tried on. There was no escape.

Her heart began to race at double-quick time, but as she watched from her window she saw Alejandro drive away, leaving his wife to walk alone into the house. It was a bitter sort of relief.

23

It took her all of five minutes to go down to Matilde's
sewing-room, five minutes to calm her racing thoughts
and still her trembling body. Although a confrontation
with Alejandro had been avoided, meeting his wife
would be as much of a trauma. How could she be civil
to the woman who had married the man she, Tanya,
loved?

Matilde smiled as she walked in and made introductions in her very rapid Spanish, as always speaking so
quickly that one word ran into another and Tanya had
no real idea what she had said the woman's name
was — not that she needed to be told!

As Tanya watched the dress being pinned and
adjusted she covertly studied Juanita. It was no wonder
Alejandro loved her; she was beautiful. All the girls in
Tenerife were beautiful, she had noticed, but this
woman had a serene sort of beauty that came from
within, that came with the confidence of being loved
and in love. She stood tall and proud, and the purple
and silver dress enhanced her dark Latin features, and
Tanya hated her.

'You are English?' she said to Tanya, looking at her
through the mirror, her smile wide, her teeth even and
very white, and when Tanya nodded, 'My husband —
he teach me a little English, but I do not use it often. I
have never been to England. My husband — he say it is
very cold there?'

Tanya smiled and nodded. 'Sometimes. It's our
winter now, and it was snowing when I left.'

'It is our winter too.' Juanita laughed. 'It is not so
warm, do you think?'

'To me it's very warm,' Tanya returned. 'You're so
lucky to live in a place with such a wonderful climate.'
And if it hadn't been for this attractive woman she
might have been living here herself! Her mouth tightened at the thought.

The woman frowned and turned from the mirror to
look directly at Tanya. 'Something is wrong?'

Tanya shook her head and forced a smile. 'It was just a thought, nothing important. I'm sorry. Your dress is so beautiful. Do you take part in the *carnaval* every year?'

'Yes — and sometimes my husband too, but this year he say he is too busy, too much work.'

Which accounted for the fact that he had dropped her off and not come in while the fitting took place. But he would be back, and Tanya was determined that she would not be here; she would shut herself away in her room until he had safely gone.

'You will come and see the *coso*? The *coso* is — how do you say it? The grand parade? Everything stops; even my husband, he take that day off. You can join him, if you like.'

An attack of panic quickened Tanya's heart, but somehow she managed to keep a smile pinned to her lips. 'You're very kind, but I expect I shall go with my sister.'

'Ah, your sister, yes. Matilde, she mentioned her. She lives here, is that right? She works in a hotel?'

Tanya nodded.

'She has been here in Tenerife a long time?'

'Two years, yes.'

'And you have not visited before. Why is that?'

Because the man I loved married you! The words were there inside her, aching to get out, but they would never be spoken. Surprisingly Tanya found herself liking this woman, liking her as a person in her own right, hating her only because of her association with Alejandro. 'I've been too busy,' she managed, and it was in part the truth — even if it was of her own making.

'And do you like Tenerife?'

'Very much, what little I've seen of it so far.'

'You must come and visit us. My husband and I, we will be very pleased.'

Tanya's smile grew weaker. 'You're very kind, thank

you, but I'm not sure that I'll have the time. There is so much to see and do.'

To her relief Matilde spoke, successfully putting an end to the conversation, and Juanita went behind a screen to take off the dress. Tanya wanted to make her escape, but Matilde indicated that she was going to make some coffee and would like her to join them.

For the next fifteen minutes Tanya was on tenter-hooks, and just as she thought she could successfully make her excuses she heard Alejandro's car outside and his firm rap on the door.

Matilde went to open it and Juanita spoke, though Tanya had no idea what she said. All she could think of was that any second now she was going to come face to face with Alejandro. At least she was forewarned— he would have no idea that the girl he had once had a passionate affair with was sitting talking to his wife. It would be interesting to see his reaction.

To give him his due, there was little more than a sudden jerking muscle in his jaw to give away his surprise, and probably neither of the others even noticed.

His shoulders were broader than Tanya remem-bered, his black hair slightly longer, and, although he wore an open-necked shirt and plain grey trousers, they looked designer-made, his leather shoes too. In fact everything about him screamed money. He had told her that his father was a farmer, owning huge areas of land where he grew bananas and tomatoes, and that it was his ambition to follow in his footsteps. Was this from where his wealth came?

Matilde began to make introductions, but Alejandro stopped her and presumably announced that they were already acquainted. Certainly there was surprise in the woman's eyes as she looked briefly at Tanya and back to Alejandro.

But his attention was now on Tanya, and her heart began to panic as she looked at him—as she discovered that the attraction was still there! She had never expected to feel this kind of emotion; she had been filled with hate and disillusionment for so long that she had thought all other feelings dead. It was a shock to discover that he still had some sort of power over her.

'So we meet again, Tanya.' There was no warmth in his voice, no hint of pleasure. He was aloof, distancing himself from her, which was odd, considering that at the airport he had insisted that he wanted to talk to her.

She looked into the coldness of his eyes, matching the chill with her own. 'Unfortunately, yes, and if you'll excuse me I was just about to return to my room.'

A frown appeared. 'You're staying here — with Matilde?'

'That's right,' she answered sharply, 'And so is Charlene.'

'For how long?' It was almost an accusation.

'I'm here for a month — it's my holiday. Charlene lives here permanently.'

A slight pause. 'I didn't know. Matilde's never mentioned it.'

'There's no reason why she should.' Tanya lifted her hand to remove a stray strand of hair from her face, and as she did so Alejandro's eyes went to the wedding-ring that she still wore. There was a sudden narrowing, a start of surprise, though why he should be astonished she did not know. Nine years was a long time to remain single, to hold a torch for the man she had once loved. 'Goodbye, Alejandro,' she said quietly, coolly, and with a nod to his wife and to Matilde she left the room.

To her amazement he followed. 'I think after all there is much to be said, Tanya.'

She lifted her brows. 'Really?'

His snort of anger shocked her. 'I know you no longer have any feelings for me, but——'

'But nothing,' she cut in swiftly. 'It's the whole point,

isn't it? Neither of us have any feelings; it was all over a long time ago, so what is there to say? I'm not the sort of person who harbours feelings about the past, at least not when we parted on such bad terms. I'd rather leave things as they are.'

'I'd like to know what you've been doing.'

'Really?' Her fine, well-shaped brows rose.

'You're married!' It was a statement rather than a question, almost an accusation.

Tanya was tempted to let him go on thinking it, but an innate sense of honesty made her say quietly, 'I was.'

A quick frown. 'You're divorced?'

'I'm a widow,' she replied flatly.

'Oh — I'm sorry.' His face shadowed. 'You have my condolences.'

Tanya was not sure that he meant it, and she looked at him coldly. 'Thank you.'

'And I'd still like to talk to you.'

She shook her head firmly. 'There's no point. It would be a complete waste of time. Goodbye, Alejandro.'

She did not expect him to let her go, but he did, though she was conscious of him watching her as she moved down the narrow enclosed corridor to her room.

Not until she closed the door behind her did Tanya realise that she was holding her breath, and now she dragged a deep gulp of air into her tortured lungs. It was worse than she had imagined. Over the years her anger had faded. Peter had restored her sanity, made her see that she couldn't dwell on the past forever. But what she hadn't remembered was the physical attraction. None of that had faded — he still had the power to turn her limbs to jelly whether she liked it or not.

It really would be disastrous if she saw him again. Notwithstanding the fact that he was married and unavailable, it would be torture; her body wouldn't be able to cope. Not even with Peter had she reached the heights she had scaled with Alejandro — could again if she dared let it happen. Oh, no, she must never, ever let herself be coerced into any sort of one-to-one situation.

It actually amazed her that she still felt this magnetism, this strong pull towards him. It was unreal. Everything had been killed stone-dead nine years ago — or so she had thought!

She stood at the window, and less than five minutes later saw him opening the car door for his wife, pausing a moment before he got in himself, looking back at the house, almost as though he was aware of her there behind the shutters. Tanya knew he could not see her, but instinctively stepped back, and when he had gone she gave a sigh of relief and sat down on the edge of the bed.

Later, when Charlene came home, Tanya told her all about her meeting with Alejandro. 'I could not believe it when I saw him.'

'A cruel twist of fate, I agree,' said her sister. 'And what a nerve, wanting to see you again after the way he behaved. I hope you told him where to get off.'

Tanya nodded. 'I think I made myself clear.'

'And you say the dress isn't quite ready. Do you think he'll come again?'

'Goodness, I hope not,' said Tanya. 'I'm hoping his wife will pick it up herself.'

'Perhaps she doesn't drive.'

Tanya closed her eyes. 'Whatever happens, I'm going to keep well out of his way.'

But it didn't turn out like that. A few days later Matilde's daughter-in-law went into labour, complications set in, and Matilde was off like a shot to be with her family. And the very same afternoon Alejandro arrived to pick up his wife's dress.

Tanya opened the door without even thinking that it might be him, and when their eyes met her jaw sagged. 'I'm sorry; Señora Guerra's not at home.' She looked at him coldly, her tone distant. 'You'll have to come back some other time; I don't know whether the dress is ready or not.'

'Fate moves in mysterious ways.'

Her brows rose characteristically. 'You think it's fate that's throwing us together?'

'It would seem that way.'

She let out a little cry of fury. 'It seems more like a curse to me. I'll tell Matilde you called.'

But his foot was inside the door before she could stop him. 'Matilde wouldn't be very pleased if she knew you were shutting me out of her house.' His jaw was taut, his eyes glacial.

'Matilde doesn't know the circumstances.'

'I was compelled to tell her a little; she was puzzled as to how we knew each other.'

And your wife, she wanted to ask, did she hear your explanation too? Has she found out that I'm the girl you once had an affair with? The one you wrote to her about? Not that she had ever truly believed him. Her mouth was tight, her eyes mutinous. 'I don't care what Matilde might think. I don't want you here; I have nothing to say to you.'

'Were you happy in your marriage?'

The question took her by surprise, and she relaxed her grip on the door. Instantly Alejandro pushed his way inside. Tanya followed, leaving the door open, feeling that at least she had an escape route should she need it.

'You haven't answered my question.' His abrupt tone made her look at him sharply.

'Of course I was happy. I was very much in love with Peter.'

'More than you loved me?'

The directness of his question made her gasp. 'I never loved you.'

His eyes narrowed. 'You gave a very good imitation of it.'

'Did I?' she asked coldly. 'You must have been mistaken. As far as I was concerned all we were having was a brief affair, fun while it lasted. I always knew you'd be coming back here.' Lies, all lies. Goodness, how could she say such a thing?

'So it meant nothing to you.'

'No.' The obsidian darkness of his eyes unnerved her, and her answer came out in a husky whisper. She covered her embarrassment by turning it into a cough.

'And the moment my back was turned you found yourself another man and got married?'

He made it sound as though she had done it the very next day, but she wasn't going to deny it. 'Something like that.'

He shook his head, looking at her with an intentness that cut right through her. 'I never thought you were that kind of girl.'

And she hadn't thought he was the sort of man who would use a girl and then let her down with no compunction whatsoever. 'It looks as though we never really knew each other.'

He nodded. 'It certainly does.'

'And now we've sorted that out perhaps you'll go. You'll have to call again for the dress.'

'What's the hurry?' He smiled faintly, grimly, and sat in Matilde's rocking-chair.

Alarm bells rang in Tanya's head. 'Aren't you a busy man?'

'Not so much that I can't spare the odd hour to talk to an old — flame.'

He said the word sneeringly, and Tanya bridled. At the same time she could not help noticing how much better his command of the English language was. He had scarcely an accent now, and she wondered whether he had been back to England or whether he had English friends here. Whatever, he was certainly very good.

'Perhaps the "old flame" doesn't want to talk to you,' she returned acidly.

'You have other plans? You're going out, is that it? Sightseeing all by yourself. What a pity your sister is working while you're here on holiday. It cannot be much fun.'

His derogatory tone needled Tanya, and she looked at him hotly. 'Charlene has already taken one week off. I'm not complaining; I have several trips organised and——'

'But none for today?' he cut in swiftly. 'Why don't you sit down?'

Tanya sat, not because she wanted to, but because she needed to. The effect of seeing Alejandro, talking to him, trying to ignore the very real sensations that churned inside, was very debilitating.

'Is your sister still in the hotel trade?'

'Indeed. She's managing a hotel in Playa de las Americas; that's why she came out here. It was too good an offer to miss, the first time she's been in complete charge. She loves it.' He confused her by flitting from subject to subject, although she knew she would far rather talk about Charlene than herself.

'And she has not married? Her career is more important to her?'

'Let's say she's never found the right man,' said Tanya, and at the age of thirty her sister was becoming more and more choosy. Tanya sometimes wondered if she would ever find anyone who would put up with her bossy, dominating nature and her strong, independent streak.

'Had you found the right man in Peter?'

Tanya swallowed hard. His questions were certainly hard-hitting, and always unexpected. 'I wouldn't have married him otherwise.' She looked at him as she spoke, trying to convince him, hiding the fact that Peter had been second-best. She hadn't admitted that at the time, but it was true. Not that she hadn't been happy — she had, very much so; he was a wonderful man — but the excitement of a strong physical relationship had been missing. If she hadn't met Alejandro she would never have known what she was capable of, what she needed, what her body needed. As it was, he had spoiled her for anyone else. She gave a tiny sigh, and Alejandro's mouth tightened, and she guessed he thought she was sighing for Peter.

'I thought I was seeing a ghost when I spotted you at the airport,' he said, with another complete turn in the conversation.

'I wasn't too happy about seeing you either,' she retorted.

'I didn't say I didn't want to see you.' The frown was there, grooving his brow, narrowing his eyes. 'It had been so long, I'd given up the idea that we'd ever meet again.'

And whose fault was that? she wanted to ask. You were the one who went away without a word; you were the one who ended it all. She lifted her shoulders in a tiny careless gesture. 'It's a small world. Would you like a cup of coffee?' She had to get out of the room, away from the stifling atmosphere. She had never known it would be like this.

'No, thank you,' he answered. 'I'd much prefer to sit and talk to you.'

Tanya groaned inwardly. 'About what? What is there to say? I'm sure you're not interested in every single little detail of my life since we parted, and neither do I want to hear about yours.'

Her bitter tone caused a further tightening of his features. 'You're making it pretty plain what you think about me.'

'There's no point in pretending.'

'I really misjudged you, Tanya.' He stood up suddenly, abruptly.

Good, he was going. Tanya rose too, but somehow they bumped into each other, and the next moment she was in his arms, his mouth on hers, and the years in between might never have been.

She was conscious of nothing except a rising hunger inside her, a desire that had lain buried for so many years. Nothing had changed. It was sheer insanity, she knew, but as her mouth clung to his the rights and wrongs of the situation did not seem to matter.

And she sensed in him the same voracity, felt him trembling slightly, felt the hammer beats of his heart, the urgency of his kisses. She began to soar, to forget the empty years. This was now, this was Alejandro, this was the man she. . .

Her thoughts tailed away. She had almost said 'loved', and that wasn't right. She did not love him. She desired him, that was all. It was a fatal attraction. Knowing him had brought her nothing but unhappiness. The trouble was she could not stop these feelings that overwhelmed her.

She had never thought of herself as being highly sexed; in fact it was only this man she responded to in such a way. Even as her thoughts ran along these lines her lips parted and their tongues entwined and she felt a powerful emotion tighten the pit of her stomach. She urged her body against his and found him equally excited, and the thought struck her that if they weren't careful they would end up making love.

It was enough to bring her to her senses, but almost as though the thought had hit him at the same time Alejandro let her go, pushing her away, and when she saw the harshness on his face she reeled back.

'What the hell's this all about, Tanya?' His voice rasped into the silence of the room. 'You declare you feel nothing for me, that you never have, and yet you kiss me like a thirsty woman who's found water in the desert. I'd like an explanation.'

Tanya closed her eyes. What could she say? She was horrified, mortified, totally ashamed of herself. What had come over her? How could she have been so wanton?

His hands snapped over her shoulders, fingers hurting, bruising. 'Look at me, Tanya. I want the truth.'

There was fire in his eyes, but ice also, a dangerous brilliance that sent a quiver of fear through her limbs. But she had no intention of letting him see that he intimidated her. 'I might ask the same of you,' she said fiercely, jerking herself free. Goodness, he was a married man; didn't that mean anything to him?

'I've always found you irresistible.'

'So that's what it was all those years ago?' she snapped. 'Sheer lust! The taking of a body that was only too willing!'

A shadow crossed his eyes, as though she had touched a raw nerve, gone in an instant, the accusation back. 'And how about you? Are you as guilty of the same feelings that you accuse me of? Is that why you responded now, why you responded to me when I was in England?'

'Unfortunately, yes,' she rasped, deciding honesty was the best policy. 'But it's not something I'm proud of, and I certainly have no intention of letting it happen again.'

'We might not be able to help ourselves.'

'You speak as though we're likely to meet again. I can assure you we will not; I shall make very certain of that.'

Again that narrowing of his eyes, an intent look that pierced right through her, a muscle jerking in his jaw. He shook his head slowly. 'You've changed, Tanya.'

'Doesn't life change us all? It deals some bitter blows; it's impossible to remain the same. My values have definitely changed.'

'It's sad to be widowed so young, certainly, but you shouldn't let it affect you forever. Life has to go on; you have to enjoy yourself again.' There was a sudden, surprising softness to his tone.

Tanya was glad he had misconstrued her words; no way did she want him to think that he was the one who had hurt her when he left England so suddenly and unexpectedly. 'I intend to,' she said, 'But in my own way — and that does not involve you. I'm not interested in rekindling our affair.'

The telephone ringing cut short their conversation.

'You'd better answer it,' said Tanya. 'I can't cope with the language.'

In the event it turned out to be Charlene. Tanya heard Alejandro explaining who he was and what he was doing there, and then Charlene must have given him a piece of her mind, because his face was grim when he turned back to Tanya and handed her the receiver. 'Your sister.' And when she had finished her conversation he said tightly, 'Is this a mutual hatred society? I was told in no uncertain terms to keep clear of you. What have you said to poison her mind against me?'

'I didn't have to say anything,' replied Tanya, her chin lifting haughtily. 'My sister is naturally very protective of me.'

His brows rose. 'I can assure you you need no protection; you're more than capable of looking after yourself.'

'I agree,' she said. 'And as a person who is very much in charge of her life, I'd like to ask you to leave.'

'What if I say I'd like that coffee now?'

'I'd say you were too late; the offer's withdrawn.'

'In that case,' he said with a shrug of his wide shoulders, 'I appear to have no choice, but this won't be the last time we meet, Tanya; I can guarantee that.'

CHAPTER THREE

IN THE days that followed Tanya was on tenterhooks. She did not want to see Alejandro again, but she did not see how she could avoid him if he came to the house. Matilde still had not returned, staying to look after her new grandchild while her daughter-in-law recovered from her ordeal, although Charlene had said that Matilde was using this as an excuse. The truth was she loved babies.

Tanya could have gone out every single moment of every single day, but she did not want to feel pushed into doing something simply because of Alejandro. When she had first said she was coming out here Charlene had said she would try and get the whole month off, but Carlos, her under-manager, had gone off sick and no one else was capable of taking over, and so Tanya was left to her own devices. She could have hired a car, but decided it wouldn't be very exciting driving around by herself.

It was a pity in one way that Charlene had chosen to live so far away from the beaches and the lively tourist areas. On the other hand, she saw the real Tenerife; she could wander into the village, where the pace of life was slow, watch the men talking over their drinks outside the local bar, the children playing, the dogs scavenging. Her disadvantage was the language barrier. The children could say hello and goodbye; their parents spoke no English at all.

Charlene had taken her into Playa de las Americas and Los Cristianos, and she had seen how the concrete jungle of tourism skirted the southern shore, and had experienced for herself the frenetic pace, even though people were supposed to be on holiday. At heart,

Tanya was a country lover and wanted to explore the unspoilt parts of the island, but not on her own.

One night Charlene drove her to a restaurant in the mountains high on the west coast, close to Masca. Tanya had been looking forward to it all day, but when their route took them along a series of extremely narrow and tight hairpin bends winding through the mountain like goat tracks, she began to wonder whether it was a good idea. And upon arrival she was horrified to discover Alejandro's dark red Mercedes parked outside. She wanted to turn right round and go home.

'Not on your life,' exclaimed Charlene. 'Not after I've driven all this way. Don't worry, I'll protect you.'

'I don't need your protection,' retorted Tanya. 'I'm twenty-seven, not seven. But this place is so out of the way; I cannot believe I'm about to bump into him again.'

'It has a good reputation,' informed her sister, 'And, judging by the number of cars, it's already busy. Perhaps with a bit of luck he won't even see us.'

But luck wasn't with them. The second they walked out on to the purple and red bougainvillaea-covered terrace perched on the mountainside Tanya saw Alejandro. Her heartbeats quickened, her throat tightened, and she looked across at his companion, giving a start of surprise when she discovered that it was not his wife.

The woman had black hair, the same, but it was short and thick and cut on a level with her chin. She wore a white low-cut dress and a chunky green necklace and was beautiful in a different sort of way to Juanita. She had eyes only for her companion, her hand touching his arm across the table in a proprietorial, familiar gesture.

Tanya felt her blood begin to boil. He was two-timing his wife *again*! Although he hadn't been married when he was in England, it amounted to the same thing. What a swine, what a cheat, what a bastard! How many other women had he had affairs with? At that moment he looked up and saw her.

If looks could kill he should have dropped dead; instead he offered her a surprised smile. Tanya glared icily and turned to her sister, who had been frantically looking for an empty table. 'There don't seem to be any,' she muttered. 'We ought to have booked.'

'Then let's get out of here,' hissed Tanya. 'I've just seen Alejandro—and he's with another woman.'

'Where?' Charlene scanned the room, and at the same time Alejandro rose from his table and came over to them.

His easy smile belied the fact that he had been caught deceiving his wife. 'As there are no tables perhaps you'd care to join us.'

'Like hell we would,' hurled Tanya. 'We'll find somewhere else to eat. It would be criminal to spoil your *pleasure*.'

Her deliberate emphasis on the last word caused a swift frown of annoyance. 'You're being extremely childish, Tanya. Inocente and I would be more than pleased to have your company.'

Inocente! Tanya glanced across at the black-haired girl and thought, Who are you trying to fool? This girl in no way wanted their presence at the table; it was there in her expression, in the hostility in her eyes, and Tanya could not believe it when Charlene accepted gracefully.

'Thank you, Alejandro. I really did want Tanya to experience this place.'

He gave a pleased smile and led the way back to their corner table. 'What did you do that for?' Tanya whispered fiercely to her sister as she trailed behind. 'This is the last thing I want.'

Charlene grinned. 'I thought it would be fun to ruin his evening.'

And ruin mine too, thought Tanya, though she relaxed a mite. Charlene's evil pleasure was infectious.

Introductions were made and the dark-haired girl smiled, though it was a surface smile only. She clearly wished them a thousand miles away, and must have wondered why her companion had insisted on inviting them to their table.

Inocente's English was good, and she listened attentively while Alejandro explained how he had met Tanya and Charlene, though her eyes were sharp as she looked from one sister to the other, evidently wondering whether either of them had been his lover.

A waiter came and set their places, handing each of them a menu, enquiring whether they would like an aperitif. Charlene declined, and Alejandro offered Tanya some of their wine. It was an excellent Marqués de Cáceres red, and Tanya drank half of it straight away, needing the courage it would give her to get through the rest of the evening. Alejandro raised an eyebrow and topped up her glass.

It was not easy to concentrate on the menu; she was far too aware of Alejandro at her side. She and her sister had effectively split him and his companion up. Inocente remained opposite him, while she and Charlene were opposite each other. Tanya knew that Alejandro always liked his girlfriend to sit facing him so that he could look at her while they ate and talked, but the way it had turned out this evening Tanya wished she hadn't been forced to sit so close.

'I certainly never expected to see you two here tonight,' said Alejandro.

I bet you didn't, she wanted to scream. I bet you thought you'd be nice and safe here in this out-of-the-way place. Her eyes flashed daggers, but somehow she managed to keep her tone even. 'We seem to be meeting a lot in unexpected circumstances.'

'Indeed we do.'

His leg brushed hers as he spoke, maybe accidentally, maybe not. Tanya quickly tucked her feet beneath her chair. He was the world's worst louse, she decided, and yet, despite her adverse feelings, she could not ignore the very real triggers of sensation that chased through her. Even knowing he was deceiving his wife, she still felt an incredible awareness. She was no better than the girl sitting next to her, she concluded angrily. 'It's strange that Charlene's been here for two years and you've not met, and now I've come we seem to be bumping into each other all the time.'

'Very strange,' he admitted, and then in a voice so low neither of the others heard, 'Or kismet.'

Tanya wanted to yell at him, to ask him what the devil he thought he was doing. Casanova had nothing on him. But she did not want to cause a scene in the restaurant and so she pretended not to have heard, and when the waiter came for their order she turned to him with relief.

It was a very long, tense next few hours. Inocente kept trying to dominate Alejandro's attention, but he insisted on bringing Tanya and Charlene into the conversation, and in the end the Tinerfeño girl lapsed into sullen silence.

Charlene insisted on talking about Tanya's husband, Peter. 'They were so much in love,' she concluded.

Tanya had tried to tell her sister to shut up by flashing her messages with her eyes, but Charlene either did not see or did not want to see, and by the end of the evening tempers were beginning to get short all round—except for Charlene's; she was thoroughly enjoying the situation. She could see by the tightening of Alejandro's face that he did not want to hear about Peter, but deliberately went on stressing his and Tanya's perfect relationship.

Tanya was glad when it was all over, when they pushed back their chairs and stood up to leave, though not so happy when Alejandro insisted on settling their bill. It made her feel indebted to him, and she did not want that; she did not want to feel any obligation whatsoever.

'I wish you hadn't said anything about Peter,' she said crossly to her sister as they made their way back down the mountain. Alejandro had sped off in front of them and was already well out of sight.

Charlene grimaced cheerfully. 'It's what he deserves. I hope it put him strictly in his place; the man's dissolute. I wonder if Inocente knows he's married. I felt like telling her, except that I didn't want to cause a scene, and I'm certainly glad that it all ended between you two. Imagine if you'd married him and he carried on like this.'

Tanya had already thought of that. The person she felt sorry for was Juanita. 'I guess that was never on the cards. I was just one of many.'

There must have been something in her voice that gave her away, because Charlene looked at her sharply. 'Hey, you're not still carrying a torch for him?'

'Charlene! Keep your eyes on the road,' screeched Tanya as they veered dangerously close towards the edge. The mountainside dropped sharply away and there were no barriers.

'Whoops!' exclaimed her sister, correcting the car. 'But if you do feel something for Alejandro, then you'd better get rid of it straight away. That man is bad news without a doubt.'

'You don't have to tell me,' replied Tanya, 'I know exactly what he's like, and don't worry, I have no intention of getting involved with him again. I learned my lesson a long time ago.' She closed her eyes as Charlene negotiated another sharp bend. This wasn't her idea of fun at all. She hadn't enjoyed it coming up, but it was even more scary going down, especially when all they had to guide them was the moon and the stars. Charlene seemed to have no qualms, but as far as she was concerned it was distinctly perilous.

They lapsed into silence, and she could not get

Alejandro out of her mind. She kept thinking of him with Inocente while his wife sat unsuspectingly at home. There was no doubt that he was having an affair with the girl; it was there in the way she looked at him, the way he spoke to her, the way they had walked out to his car with their arms around each other. Tanya felt quite sick at the thought.

When they got back home she feigned tiredness and went straight to her room. It had been bad enough discovering that she had meant nothing to Alejandro all those years ago, but to find out that he was still two-timing Juanita was devastating in the extreme. She had never thought in those early days that Alejandro was a womaniser. It was hard to believe that he had set out on this treacherous path of deceit at the early age of twenty-three. The saying that a leopard never changed its spots was certainly true where he was concerned. She wondered how many other girls there had been.

The next day Matilde came home and Alejandro turned up to collect the dress. This time Tanya had been half expecting him, knowing that he would want to make some sort of excuse for the night before.

She was outside when he came, sitting on a chair in the tiny square of back garden, soaking up the sunshine, Matilde's tan and white dog keeping her company, although he lay in the shade of the wall. She was out of sight of the front door, and although she had heard Alejandro's car had thought herself relatively safe. Until she heard him call her name.

Ought she to pretend not to hear? Her stomach muscles clenched involuntarily, pulses jerked, and she knew there was no way she could ignore him. Like him or hate him, it was all the same; the animal magnetism was there — getting stronger by the day!

Slowly she turned her head. 'Señora Guerra's in the house.' Her tone was hard, belying her tumultuous feelings.

'I'd like a word with you first.' He pushed open the gate and strode the few feet to her side.

'If it's about last night I don't want to hear.' There was irritation in her tone, and her sloe-shaped blue eyes were cold and distant. 'You'll never change, will you, Alejandro?' He loomed over her, tall and somehow threatening, putting her at a distinct disadvantage. She jumped to her feet and faced him.

He frowned. 'What are you talking about?'

'Don't come the innocent with me,' she cried. 'How many other women have there been?'

'Other women?'

'Yes, affairs on the side. It's a good job you didn't bring your wife along today or I might have been tempted to tell her.' Fury added strength to her words, and she was speaking much more loudly than she intended. Matilde popped her head out of the door, frowned in their direction, and disappeared again.

Tanya was so uptight that she missed the shadow that crossed Alejandro's face, saw only the tightening of his jaw, the suppression of his anger. 'My words have struck home, have they?'

'You don't know what you're talking about, Tanya.' His normally generous lips were clamped thinly, his dark eyes as hard as polished jet.

'Don't I?' She lifted her fine brows and eyed him coldly. 'How can I not know when you flaunt your girlfriends under everyone's nose?'

'You're talking about Inocente?'

'That's right.'

'And Beatriz, I presume?'

Tanya frowned. 'Beatriz? Who's she?'

'You seem to think that she's my girlfriend too,' he rasped coldly. 'Can you tell me what gave you that idea?'

'If you're talking about the woman whose dress Matilde's making, I didn't think she was your girlfriend,' snapped Tanya. 'I thought she was your wife, but if she isn't then you're simply confirming my already rock-bottom opinion of you.'

He looked at her sharply, questioningly. 'You'd heard I was married?'

'Yes, I had.' Tanya's tone was bitter. 'And I think what you're doing to her is diabolical. You want stringing up.'

'When did you hear? How did you hear?' He seemed not to notice her harsh words.

'Is it important?' she snapped.

'I'd like to know.' His eyes were narrowed on hers, his expression unreadable.

Tanya lifted her shoulders in a careless gesture. 'Someone Charlene met in the hotel told her. He came from Tenerife, knew you, apparently.'

'Was this before or after you'd married Peter?'

Suddenly she could see the way his mind was working. 'Heavens,' she cried sharply, 'I didn't marry him on the rebound, if that's what you're thinking. I didn't marry him because I'd heard you'd got married; it was a long time afterwards. And as Charlene said last night, we were extremely happy together. I would never have dreamt of seeing another man behind his back.'

She was so indignant that she was out of breath, her chest heaving as she looked at him belligerently and coldly, her fingers curled into her palms so tightly that her nails dug in and hurt, but she did nothing about it; in fact she welcomed the pain.

His eyes glittered with a cold light that Tanya had never seen before; his nostrils dilated. 'After all we had going for us, Tanya, I would never have believed that you could think so harshly of me.'

'All we had going for us?' she echoed loudly. 'We had nothing. It was a brief, glorious fling that was over the moment you left England.' And she was lying again! But what the hell—she refused to succumb to the indignity of confessing that she had spent hours and hours crying, pining, longing, wondering.

'You forgot me so instantly?'

His expression was so incredulous that she almost laughed. 'Indeed I did. What did you expect? It was fun while it lasted, I admit, but once you were out of sight, Alejandro, you were out of mind. And why am I telling you all this when it's your wife who's the person I feel sorry for? You really are a swine, aren't you? What do you tell her—that it's business keeping you away from home? Or have you some other fancy excuses?'

Alejandro looked at her long and hard. 'I hardly feel you deserve the truth.'

'Truth?' Tanya's brows slid up. 'You mean a pack of lies? Some way of attempting to absolve yourself? I don't think I want to hear it.' He had lied by omission nine years ago, proving he wasn't a man of integrity. Why should she believe anything he tried to tell her now? And lord, she wished he would move. Her hostility was mixed with an awareness that was proving a very real threat to her sanity.

'In that case there is nothing else I have to say.' He turned abruptly and marched towards the house, and perversely Tanya wished she hadn't been so sharp. It would have been interesting to hear what sort of an excuse he came up with. It was too late now, though. Matilde had appeared in the doorway and was beaming a smile of welcome. He was obviously a great favourite of hers.

Tanya sat down again and closed her eyes. She looked completely relaxed, as though she hadn't a care in the world, no hint on her face of her rioting body and mind. Not only was she battling with a desire to know what he had been going to say, but she was struggling with feelings that set her on fire, feelings she had thought long since dead. Why, when she knew only too well how immoral he was, did she respond like this? What was there about him that drew her like a moth to a flame?

He had said that it was kismet that drew them together and she had scorned the idea, but was there something in it? Why, after all these years apart, had they met again like this? Each occasion had been accidental — at the airport, the first time he came here, last night. Was there truly some hidden force behind it? Was it their destiny?

He obviously wasn't happy with his wife or he wouldn't be seeking the company of other women. On the other hand, he hadn't exactly been true to her before their marriage. He was a philanderer, a Don Juan, a man to be avoided at all costs. How many hearts he had broken she hated to think. Hers had been shattered. It had taken years to find the pieces and put it back together, and she was darn sure she wasn't going to risk it being damaged again.

It seemed an age that he remained indoors with the older woman. Tanya wondered whether he would come and speak to her once more or whether he would leave by the front door and that would be an end to it. She hoped for the latter, and since the costume was ready he would have no excuse for calling again.

She heard them talking, Matilde sounding excited, Alejandro's deep voice amused, and they were coming towards her. Tanya knew she could not pretend to be asleep, so she opened her eyes as they drew near.

Alejandro looked down at her. 'I've just given Matilde her usual invitation to our annual masked ball — well, maybe "ball" is too grand a word, it's a party really; everyone has them around *carnaval* time — and she thought it would be nice if you and your sister came too.'

Tanya's heartbeats grew heavy and rapid, her eyes widened, and she looked quickly from one to the other. Matilde was nodding and smiling, and Tanya could see that she genuinely wanted them to accompany her. Alejandro had no expression at all on his face.

'It's not really up to Matilde, is it?' she asked a trifle sharply.

Alejandro gave a wry smile. 'In that case, the invitation comes directly from me. Would you and Charlene do me the pleasure of attending?'

Tanya wanted to say no, definitely not, but she did not want to offend Matilde, who obviously thought it a brilliant idea. Besides, it would give her the opportunity to find out where Alejandro lived—she was curious about that—and what sort of a lifestyle he had, and—more interestingly—whether he had invited any other ex- or current girlfriends. 'I'll have to ask Charlene first,' she countered.

'Naturally, but I'm sure she won't refuse.'

'She might be working. When is it?'

'On Saturday—and I'm sure she'll be able to re-arrange her schedule if necessary.'

'Maybe,' Tanya said with a shrug.

'I think Matilde would welcome you accompanying her.'

'Do you always invite her?'

'Of course; my family have known her for many years.'

'Does she usually accept?'

He grimaced. 'Not always, which is a pity. It is one way we can repay her for all the long hours she puts in for us during the year. She not only makes costumes for our family for the *carnaval*, but she does all our dressmaking, and any necessary repairs and alterations. She is a—what do you say—a gem. One in a million.'

He was making it very hard for them to refuse, and probably knew it, because there was a confident smile on his lips.

'I'll still have to ask Charlene,' she said.

'As far as I'm concerned, her acceptance is a fore-gone conclusion. I'll expect you about eight-thirty. And don't forget to wear your mask—it's part of the fun.'

He kissed Matilde warmly on the cheek and made

his way back out of the gate. The tiny woman looked after him with admiration. *'Maravilloso, maravilloso,'* she said, but Tanya was wondering what he meant by 'fun'.

Charlene, as she might have known, was all for the idea; she enjoyed partying, though she did have one reservation. 'Whatever you do, steer clear of Alejandro—I don't want you getting upset all over again.'

'I don't need the warning,' replied Tanya, while privately thinking it might not be so easy. She somehow could not see herself being allowed to go through the whole evening without his seeking her out, and if she had to dance with him, if their bodies were pressed close together for any length of time, it would create total havoc with her senses.

They had three days to decide what to wear, for Matilde to make their masks, and for Tanya to worry herself sick about seeing Alejandro again. On the second day she accompanied Charlene into Playa de las Americas and spent her time looking round the shops for a suitable dress.

She was not sure what would be acceptable, but in the end chose an azure voile dress that complemented the colour of her eyes. The full, layered skirt felt pretty and feminine and the sleeveless, fitted top was held up by shoelace-thin straps. It was perfect for a party and she could wear it at other times as well, which did not make it feel such an extravagance.

The day of the party dawned, and apprehension tightened Tanya's nerves. Charlene came home from work early and Matilde ordered a taxi so that they would not have to worry about drinking and driving.

Alejandro's house was much further away than Tanya expected, on the outskirts of La Orotava in the north, and the winding mountain road took them through the beautiful, lush Orotava valley. In the taxi's headlamps Tanya could see that it was moist and fertile

with trees and bushes lining the road. 'You must bring
me here in the daytime,' she said impulsively to her
sister. 'What an island of contrasts this is.'

Tanya did not know what she had expected
Alejandro's house to look like—certainly not unfinished like Matilde's, but neither had she expected it to
be this magnificent. She had vaguely imagined a large
new house; instead it was a cream-painted mansion,
hundreds of years old. She was extremely impressed,
and more so when they walked through a wrought-iron
gate into an inner tiled courtyard where a fountain
played and people mingled. It was extraordinary.

He was certainly far wealthier than she had imagined, She stood there looking around her, completely
awed. On each of the four sides were intricately carved
wooden balconies, two tiers of them, and people were
walking or talking, or looking down, and fairy-lights
were strung along the length of them and between the
shiny monster plants that grew in rich profusion in
corners of the patio, different types of palms and ferns
reaching for the sky, plants Tanya did not know the
name of. It was like another world. And everyone
wore masks and beautiful clothes, the women looking
like brilliant butterflies, their dark-suited male counter-
parts a perfect foil.

On one section of the balcony a three-piece band
played, softly, evocatively, although Tanya had no
doubt that the volume would be turned up later on in
the evening. She looked around her for Alejandro but
could not see him. She had thought, mask or no, he
would be instantly recognisable, but there were other
tall, broad-shouldered males, and he could have been
any one of them.

It was actually an exciting thought that she could
stand next to him, brush by him, and not know it was
him. On the other hand, he would not recognise her
either, and it gave her a feeling of security. She was
safe here; she could enjoy herself. She turned to speak

to her sister, but Charlene had already disappeared into the crowd, Matilde too, and she was alone here in this gathering of happy people.

She looked for Inocente and Beatriz, wondered which of the women there was Alejandro's wife, and when a pretty girl came by with a tray of drinks Tanya took one and discovered it was champagne. Her nose wrinkled. Champagne held bittersweet memories. The very first time she had tasted it was on the day she had met Alejandro at her friend's wedding reception, and ever since it had brought back memories of that moment when their eyes met and she had known he was someone special.

'You shouldn't be standing alone.'

A deep voice in her ear startled her, and for a moment she thought it was Alejandro. Her heart began to patter, but when he spoke again she wondered how she could have been so wrong.

'I'm all right; I'm enjoying it. How did you know I was English?' He looked nothing like Alejandro really; his mouth was much thinner, his nose narrower.

'I didn't; it was a guess. Are you here alone?'

'I'm with my sister and my landlady actually, but they seem to have disappeared.'

'Are you a friend of Alejandro's?'

Tanya grimaced. 'I suppose you could say that. I knew him a long time ago in England. It's some house he has here.'

'It's been in his family for generations.'

'Oh?' Tanya had thought he and Juanita had bought it when they got married, that he had moved out of the family home. She wondered whether his brothers and sisters still lived here — or whether they were married too now and had moved out. There was a lot she did not know.

'Alejandro took over when his father died. You've not been here before?'

'No, I haven't. I'm here on holiday as a matter of

fact. I bumped into Alejandro accidentally, and he invited us to his party.'

'It's something that shouldn't be missed. Would you care to dance?'

Tanya looked around the crowded courtyard, saw other couples attempting it and failing because of the sheer number of people standing around, and shook her head. 'I don't think it's possible. Maybe later?'

'Can I show you my cousin's house, then?'

'Alejandro is your cousin?' Tanya felt a sharp shock of disbelief.

'Indeed he is; our fathers were brothers. May I introduce myself? Juan Vázquez Rodriquez.'

Tanya frowned. 'Vázquez *Rodriguez*? Alejandro is Vázquez Herrera. If your fathers are brothers you would surely have the same surname?' Was this man lying to her? Was he in fact no relation at all? Was he trying to make her feel safe when his intentions were perhaps strictly dishonourable?

'It can be confusing, I agree,' he said with a smile. 'We always have two surnames; didn't Alejandro tell you that? The first one our father's, the second our mother's — hence the difference. And you, my English rose, what is your name?'

'Tanya. Tanya Elliott.'

'A beautiful name for a beautiful girl.'

Unconsciously he had repeated Alejandro's own words, and Tanya wondered if all these Canario men were so profuse with their compliments.

At that moment Charlene came bustling up. 'There you are, Tanya; I wondered where you'd got to.' The older girl wore a brilliant red dress that offset her colouring beautifully. She had tucked a red hibiscus flower into her hair, and her delicate red mask was edged with glittering red sequins. She looked very exotic.

'Is this your sister?' Juan looked at the taller girl admiringly.

Tanya nodded. 'Yes, this is Charlene. Charlene, Alejandro's cousin, Juan.'

'Alejandro's cousin?'

Tanya knew that her sister's brows would be raised enquiringly, her eyes questioning. It was amazing how much of a person's expression these masks hid.

'Indeed I am,' Juan answered immediately. 'I was just about to show Tanya around the house. It would be my pleasure if you would accompany us as well.'

'Why don't you take Charlene while I stand around here a while longer?' suggested Tanya. The truth was she was scared of running into Alejandro. She wanted to stay here in the relative anonymity of a crowd. And she had seen Juan's sudden interest in her sister.

Charlene smiled, the suggestion pleasing her too. 'An excellent idea, Come along, Juan.' And she took hold of his arm.

Tanya gave a tiny inward smile. Charlene could be very dominant; Juan might not like it. On the other hand, she might be his type of girl. Who could tell?

She stood alone, thinking, dreaming, and through the murmur of voices all around her, the clink of glasses, the subtle blend of perfumes, Tanya could feel Alejandro's presence. It was as though he stood at her side, touching her, caressing her, and her skin shivered and she moved, but the feeling remained. He was there, somewhere, watching her. He had recognised her despite the blue mask with its painted-on eyes and beads and tiny feathers which obscured the whole of her face except her mouth.

She finished her champagne and took another glass off a passing girl and tried to bury herself deeper in the crowd. It was all in her mind, of course; he could not possibly identify her, could he?

Matilde approached and Tanya gave her a relieved smile. Matilde, in her black dress and gold mask, was nevertheless instantly recognisable because she was so tiny and her hair was still taken back in its relentless bun. Tanya wondered whether she ought to have fixed her own hair differently. Would it be a give-away? Ought she to have swept it up and dressed it with combs and jewels?

I'm becoming paranoid, she thought; I must stop this at once and begin to enjoy myself. She caught sight of Charlene up on the top balcony, Juan attentive at her side. Her sister was definitely enjoying herself—and she ought to be doing the same!

When a young man asked her to dance Tanya immediately accepted, and after that she was in constant demand. Most of them spoke only a few words of English, but it did not matter, and when one of them took her inside to a table groaning under the weight of carefully prepared food she discovered that she was actually enjoying herslf, that for the last hour she had forgotten Alejandro and was now completely relaxed.

The choice was staggering: smoked eel, deep-fried squid, snails, oysters, baby octopus—lots and lots of fish dishes—chicken breasts, chicken legs, hams and venison, various goats' cheeses—ewe's milk cheese, cream cheese, hard cheese—crusty bread, fruit, stuffed olives, asparagus tips, melon, an assortment of salads, paella, omelettes—and much, much more!

And afterwards it was back to the dancing. Tanya was whirled from partner to partner and she was laughing and happy—until she felt arms much stronger than the rest pull her against a body much harder than the rest. 'I think I've waited long enough,' came the deep-throated words.

CHAPTER FOUR

TANYA saw the glitter of brown eyes behind the black mask. She must have looked at Alejandro a dozen times tonight and not recognised him—yet he had known that she was the girl in the vibrant blue dress, the dancing butterfly whose feet had hardly touched the ground. 'How did you know it was me?' she asked huskily, her heart throbbing, suddenly, painfully, her throat aching and tightening.

'I saw you arrive,' he said simply.

'You've known for three hours and done nothing about it?' He had been watching her all this time?

'Did you want to dance with me?' came the curt question. Tanya shook her head firmly.

'I thought not, but I could not let the whole evening go by without at least one dance. You look ravishing, Tanya; has anyone told you that yet?'

'Everyone,' she announced airily.

His bark of laughter was surprising. 'Then they all have good taste, but don't forget I was the first to know you.'

'This is a splendid party,' she said in an attempt to move the conversation away from themselves.

'I'm glad you're enjoying it.'

'You have a wonderful house,'

'Have you seen around it yet?'

Tanya shook her head. 'Your cousin, Juan, offered to show me, but he took Charlene instead.'

'Yes, I've seen them together.'

He seemed to know who everyone was, despite their masks, and he looked exciting in his white dinner-jacket. In fact he was the only one in white; all the other men wore more traditional black.

'If you'd like to see it, I'll show you.'

'No, thanks,' she replied quickly. 'I'm enjoying your party, but I don't want to intrude into your—private life.'

'You think my—wife would have something to say about it?'

'If it was me I wouldn't be very happy if you took other girls all over the house,' she replied tartly. She tried to put a little space between them, but his arms were like bands of iron.

'Into the bedroom, you're thinking?'

Tanya lifted her shoulders. 'Not exactly, but I've no doubt it was in your mind.' Throb, throb, went her heart, and she hoped to goodness that Alejandro could not feel it against him.

'You have a very low opinion of me.'

'With just cause, wouldn't you think?' she asked, her tone deliberately cold. 'Which one is your wife?' She looked at the other dancers, as she had all evening, trying to guess which one was Juanita.

'Let's get out of this crowd,' he said abruptly, and, taking her wrist, he led her up a set of stairs to the first balcony. There he found a corner hidden by the palms creeping their way skyward.

Tanya felt her heart panicking and wondered at his sudden decision to get her alone—and alone they were! Although she could hear countless voices, the beat of insistent music, the peal of laughter, they were as alone as if they were locked in a room. Everyone was too busy having a good time to take any notice of them in this empty corner.

Breathless at the speed with which he had brought her here, Tanya leaned back against the wall. 'What's this all about?' Still her tone was distant; she did not want to give away by the slightest breath that she was drawn magnetically to him, that none of the feelings she had experienced all those years ago had faded.

'Your constant references to my wife.' There was a hardness in his tone too, and Tanya wondered.

'It hurts you, does it, that you've been caught out?' she asked scornfully. 'Or does everyone else know about your extra-marital affairs and out of loyalty say nothing?'

Alejandro's mouth tightened. 'There are no extra-marital affairs, Tanya. Juanita died six years ago.'

Tanya felt as though she had been delivered a body-blow. Her hands went to her mouth, and she was glad he could not see the swift, embarrassed colour suffusing her cheeks. This was the last thing she had expected. 'Oh, Alejandro, I'm sorry, so sorry; why didn't you——'

'Tell you?' he cut in harshly. 'Why, when you were so busy condemning me, so eager to think the worst?'

'Can you blame me?' she asked, busy doing some mental calculations. Six years ago, was about the time she had married Peter. She winced at the irony of it.

'You should have known I'm not the type to play around behind my wife's back.'

'That's rich,' she cried. 'What were you doing with me?'

'I wasn't married then.'

'No, but Juanita was at home waiting for you. I'm sorry that she died, but I still think you're an out-and-out swine. I've seen you with two different girls already, one of them married! I stupidly thought Beatriz was talking about you when she mentioned her husband. It's beyond belief the way you behave—and if I said I'd come out with you you'd probably have no qualms about that either. The way I see things, you've always enjoyed playing the field.'

Just below the edge of his mask she saw the spasmodic jerk of a muscle, his eyes glittering through the narrow slits in the plain black velvet—not for him the glitter of sequins—and she was glad she had angered him. He deserved it. He tried to give the image of being an upper-class gentleman, but hell, he was nothing of the sort! He used people for his own perverse pleasure. God, she hated him.

'You jump to rash conclusions, Tanya. I——'

'I'm not going to listen to any excuses,' she flared. 'I know what I've seen and I don't like it, and when I get back home to England I shall push all thoughts of you out of my mind—forever.' Her chest heaved and her eyes were as bright as his.

'You think that will be possible?' he asked, a much quieter edge to his tone, a stillness about him that was somehow threatening.

'I haven't thought about you for years; why should I suddenly start thinking about you now?' she asked, unaware of the desperation in her tone.

'Because of this.' And before she could stop him, before she could even hazard a guess at his intentions, he had enfolded her into the circle of his arms and lowered his head until their two mouths met.

The last time it had happened, in Matilde's house, Tanya had been unprepared and let herself respond unthinkingly. Now she knew such a reaction would be fatal, and although it took every ounce of will-power and then some she managed to hold herself rigid. She told herself the touch of his lips meant nothing, that the racing of her heart meant nothing, that this man meant nothing.

But Alejandro was not so easily put off. Instead of letting her go, pushing her away in disgust, or even making bruising demands, he slipped off her mask and his mouth gentled, playing on hers expertly, sensually, feather-light kisses on her cheeks, her eyes, her ears, creating sensations, drawing out responses, slowly, reluctantly, until finally she felt herself drowning and could hold back no longer.

It was all and everything she remembered, sweet, sweet agony, a drawing-out of her soul, every inch of her sensitised, responsive, needing, hungering. Oh, lord, why? *Why*! Against her own better judgement she pressed her body to his, felt his own pulsing need of her. Her lips parted, his tongue explored, she groaned, he groaned, neither spoke. It was a moment of intense physical pleasure.

When she unconsciously moved against him his arms tightened, his kiss deepened, and sheer animal hunger drove them both into a frenzy of kissing and touching and feeling and exciting. Tanya had forgotten how high he made her climb; the highest peak was not impossible where this man was concerned.

He slid the thin straps off her shoulders, exposing her firm, naked, aching breasts, stroking with electric fingertips, brushing a firm thumb over sensitised nipples. Aching, longing, washed over her. Desire spread like wildfire, her fingers threading through the wiry thickness of his hair, her mouth still pressed to his, drinking from him, taking all he offered. It was bliss, sheer, sweet heaven.

The party went on around them but neither was aware of it, and when his mouth left hers to burn a trail down the arch of her throat, to move with tantalising slowness to the aching curve of her breasts, and finally to take the throbbing heart of them, to taste and nip and suck thrusting nipples into his mouth, she did nothing to stop him. She was being lifted out of herself, transported to a place where physical pleasure knew no bounds.

And that was all it was—physical—she knew, and yet she could not stop him. It was a mutual hungering of like souls; it was the sweetest torture imaginable, setting her body on fire, pulses pounding, desire coursing through each and every one of her veins.

When he raised his head to look at her his mouth was soft and wet. At some time his mask had come off too and his eyes were glazed with desire. '*Mi cariño*, he muttered thickly, '*mi cariño*. Nothing has changed. Everything is as it always was between us.'

Tanya agreed. Nothing *had* changed on a physical level. In this respect they were still compatible, still able to arouse the utmost desire in each other's bodies. It was a marvel that her hatred hadn't killed it all stone-dead, but somehow it had survived, and at this moment in time she did not want to let him go.

His mouth met hers again and she clung to him, responding with a passion that had lain dormant for too long, her lips moving over his, her tongue touching and tasting and probing. Her groin ached and she gyrated against him, needing him, wanting him, desperately, *now*! Common sense had long since flown; this man had enticed her, drugged her, made her his in every sense of the word.

'Alejandro.' She breathed his name unconsciously. 'Oh, Alejandro. . .' And her kisses deepened and her body pressed even harder into his.

He gave a groan of anguish. 'Not here, not now, *amor mio*, I see my cousin approaching, but later, yes, later we will satisfy this hunger of ours.' Deftly he straightened her dress and they both pulled on their masks. Tanya was glad of something to hide her tumultuous feelings, and when her sister and Juan drew near there was nothing in their attitude to suggest that seconds earlier they had been in a passionate embrace.

'I've been looking all over for you,' complained Charlene, glancing swiftly from one to the other. 'What are you doing here?'

'Talking about old times,' Alejandro answered, and Tanya was surprised to hear that his tone was perfectly normal. She had been afraid to speak in case she gave herself away.

'It's almost midnight,' said Juan, his arm possessively about Charlene's waist. 'Isn't that when we all unmask?'

Alejandro inclined his head. 'Usually, although I've half a mind to dispense with that this evening, let everyone go home without knowing with whom they've been dancing.'

'*Maldito sea*, Alejandro, you cannot do that,' his cousin declared tersely. 'I've had this lovely woman in my arms all evening and haven't once seen her face.'

'You expect me to believe that?' asked Alejandro with a knowing smile. 'Don't think I didn't see you disappearing into one of the bedrooms.'

'But only to show her around,' Juan defended.

Charlene nodded her agreement. 'He's been a perfect gentleman.'

'Then you're lucky,' Alejandro quipped. 'It's certainly not like the Juan I know.'

Or the Alejandro she knew, thought Tanya. He hadn't even needed the protection of four walls and a door. Anyone could have walked up and seen them. She felt suddenly mortified. How could she have let herself get so carried away?

She was glad of the few minutes' respite, and when her sister and Juan began walking away she followed. Alejandro, however, had other ideas. His hand tightened around her wrist. 'Are you forgetting we have unfinished business?' The thickness was back in his voice.

Tanya shook her head, her eyes defensive. 'I got carried away; it was a mistake, and letting you make love to me would be an even worse one.'

Nostrils flared beneath the black mask. 'You cannot deny the chemistry between us.'

'I can't deny it,' she agreed, 'But I can fight it.'

'But why, when it gives us so much pleasure?'

'Because there's more to life than lust,' she slammed back, 'and that's all it is, all it has ever been. If you must know, I'm deeply ashamed. Just keep away from me, Alejandro. I don't want you, or your body, or any part of you.' She turned and raced after her sister, but Charlene was already out of sight.

Tanya could not find her way back. The stairs

seemed to have disappeared. She tried a couple of doors, but they were locked; when she finally found one open she tumbled inside—only to discover that it was Alejandro's bedroom. At least she assumed it was his. It was a male room anyway, with heavy dark furniture and strong browns and greens in the décor. An open adjoining door revealed a stark white bathroom and the unmistakable odour of Alejandro's aftershave.

She had paused too long. Alejandro joined her, a smile of satisfaction curving his lips. 'I'm glad to see you've changed your mind.'

He knew she hadn't, he knew it was accidental her being here, but nevertheless he intended to take full advantage of the situation. At least that was Tanya's interpretation, and she glared at him angrily. 'I would never do anything so foolish. I'm trying to find my way downstairs.'

'There's no rush,' he answered quietly, his hands on her shoulders as he came up behind her.

Tanya tensed but did not move. She wanted to prove to him that he could touch her without her melting in his arms—or was it herself she wanted to convince? Whatever, it was something she had to do.

He brushed away her hair from the back of her neck and nuzzled her nape with his mouth, triggering off an instant response. Tanya clenched her teeth and tried to ignore the sensations surging through her, but when his hands slid over her shoulders and down her arms, when he turned her gently to face him, every good intention faded.

He disposed of both their masks, his eyes never leaving hers, and when he cupped her face between firm brown hands her lips parted willingly for his kiss. She was a weak-minded fool, and knew it, and yet could do nothing about it. He had some fatal hold over her; it was as though he had at some time hypnotised her and whenever he gave the signal she was his to do with as he liked.

What would have happened had someone else not made the same mistake and come tripping into his room Tanya did not know, but she took the opportunity to make her escape, following the couple out to an inner landing and down the stairs to the courtyard below.

Relief made her limbs begin to tremble, and she was leaning against one of the wooden columns that supported the balconies, listening to the drum of her heartbeats, when Alejandro caught up with her yet again. But before he could retort a dainty hand touched his arm. 'Is that you, Alejandro? I've been looking for you all night.'

Tanya recognised Inocente the moment she spoke. The girl was wearing a silver lamé figure-hugging dress which flared out just below the knee. It was dramatic and sexy and her mask was silver too, her only touch of colour the blood-red of her lipstick and the matching polish on her nails.

Alejandro turned to the girl and smiled, easily, warmly, and draped his arm casually over her shoulders, 'You're not supposed to recognise me.'

'But I'm lonely; I want you. You haven't danced with me all evening.'

'You've not been short of partners.'

So he had recognised her as well, thought Tanya.

'No, but—they're not *you*.' There was a petulant pout to the girl's lips. 'Please dance with me now.'

She tugged him away, and Tanya told herself she was relieved, yet her body still ached for him. It was sheer contrariness, and she was intensely angry with herself for allowing these base feelings to take precedence, and made a silent vow never to let it happen again.

She looked at him now, dancing with Inocente, their bodies swaying together to the seductive music, the girl's head resting against Alejandro's shoulder, his arms about her, looking for all the world like two contented lovers.

From somewhere a clock struck midnight. Everyone stopped dancing, and Alejandro stepped into the middle of the floor by the fountain. Tanya had no idea what he was saying, but everyone listened attentively, and all of a sudden masks were taken off and there were oohs and aahs and looks of surprise.

Tanya caught sight of Charlene and Juan. He was looking at her sister in undisguised admiration, and he too was more handsome than Tanya had imagined. She hoped, for Charlene's sake, that he turned out to be a better catch than his cousin.

She looked for Alejandro, saw him once again with Inocente, the girl's eyes shining, happy now that she was in the arms of the man she loved. And over there was Beatriz with her husband; at least Tanya assumed it was her husband. Alejandro stopped and said a few words to them before carrying on with Inocente around the stone-paved floor.

He was so cool about it all, thought Tanya, flaunting one girl in front of another, heedless of hurt feelings, intent only on having a good time. She looked around for Matilde and Charlene. It was time to go; she had had enough. But her sister had disappeared and Matilde was huddled in a corner, talking to another couple, looking as though she would be there for some time.

At that moment she was asked if she would like to dance, and for the next hour she was swung from partner to partner, laughing and flirting, putting it on even more when she saw Alejandro watching. It was a convincing act, yet in truth she was as miserable as sin and wished she had stuck to her guns and not let herself be persuaded to come here.

All she had found out, apart from the fact that he was a widower, was that Alejandro was as lustful as

ever and she—to her disgust—still responded to him.
She was as bad as him in fact—except that she did not
go around having affairs with several people at the
same time. Since Peter there had been no one, at least
no one of count. The odd date, yes, but nothing more
than that.

It seemed like forever before Charlene and Matilde
sought her out and said it was time they left. The crowd
was thinning, several others having already gone, and
Tanya would have liked it if they could have hopped
into their taxi without seeing Alejandro again.

Of course that was impossible, and would have been
extremely rude. In fact he approached them when he
saw them all together. 'Not leaving already?'

'It's after two,' said Charlene. 'Matilde's almost dead
on her feet, But it's been a wonderful party; thank you
very much for inviting us.'

Wonderful because she had met Juan, thought
Tanya. Matilde too was giving him her thanks, and
finally he turned to her, taking both her hands in his.
'And thank you, too, Tanya, for coming.'

'It's been quite an experience,' she said with a faint
smile. 'You certainly know how to do things in a big
way.'

'The *carnaval* is the highlight of our year; everyone
celebrates, and you certainly mustn't miss the grand
parade. In fact you mustn't miss any of it. Next week
the various dancing groups will be judged, and of
course the *reina del carnaval*, the carnival queen, will
be picked. I'm actually an honoured member of the
jury this year. I'd like you to come and watch—the
costumes they wear are out of this world. It's televised,
of course, but it's much better to be present and feel
the atmosphere.'

Tanya shook her head. 'I don't think so.'

'It's a woman's prerogative to change her mind.'

'You're asking too much.'

'It's for old times' sake.'

'Old times mean nothing to me,' she insisted.

His lips tightened in sudden anger. 'The choice is yours. I'll be in touch.'

CHAPTER FIVE

No ONE got up early on Sunday, not even Matilde, who was always an early riser. In fact Tanya was the first to get out of her bed, and only then because she'd had a restless night and could not stop thinking about Alejandro. In fact the longer she lay there, the more tormented her thoughts became.

She needed to be up and doing something, although there was very little to do in someone else's house when you were on holiday. She made herself a cup of coffee and took it outside, fussed Matilde's dog, refilled his bowl with water, and marvelled at yet another day with clear blue skies.

Charlene had suggested they go for a ride to Icod today to look at the three-thousand-year-old dragon tree and then on to Puerto de la Cruz. 'Puerto is much more sophisticated than Americas,' Charlene had told her, 'and although it has no beach as such it has a wonderful lido with a series of eight swimming-pools as well as a huge artificial lake.'

Tanya had agreed it sounded fascinating.

'And on an island in the middle of the lake is a subterranean nightclub,' Charlene had continued enthusiastically, 'All designed by César Manrique, Lanzarote's celebrated artist and architect. Everything he designs is made to look as natural as possible; the man's a genius.'

But when Charlene finally got up she announced that Juan was picking her up instead. 'I don't know why I forgot our plans,' she said apologetically. 'It must have been the drink — all that champagne, and I had a few gin and tonics as well. I don't know what I was thinking of, arranging to go out with him when you're here on holiday. Come with us; I'm sure he won't mind.'

But Tanya had no intention of playing gooseberry. She was glad Charlene had found herself a male friend, but she did wish her sister had thought more about her. In another two weeks she would be gone and Charlene could spend as much time as she liked with Juan Vázquez Rodriguez.

As it turned out Juan did not come alone; he brought with him his brother, Manuel. 'I could not let you sit here all day by yourself,' he said to Tanya as he introduced them, and the day turned out much better than she expected. Manuel was friendly and attentive, though younger than Tanya. He was a lot of fun and seemed attracted to her, even though she made it clear she was not looking for romance.

When he suggested taking her out the next day, saying it was his day off from work, she instantly accepted. A diversion like this was just what she needed to take her mind off Alejandro.

Much to Tanya's surprise he arrived on a motorbike, and her day turned out to be a hair-raising ride all around the island. It was fun, if a bit frantic at times, and she saw far more than she would have done had she waited for Charlene to take her. In fact she thoroughly enjoyed herself.

'Can I see you again?' he asked eagerly, when he finally dropped her off.

Tanya nodded. 'So long as you realise it's all just fun.' She had an idea this young man was getting serious about her. 'I don't wish to become involved.'

'There is someone else?' he asked with a frown. 'Juan said you were — what was the expression he used? Footloose and fancy-free. I am not sure what that means, but —'

'It means there is no man in my life at the moment,' Tanya informed him, 'and I want it to remain that way.'

'But why?'

'Losing my husband was painful; I'm not yet ready to start again with a new relationship.' It was a lie, but a necessary one. It was the kindest way to put this boy off.

'I understand,' he said, 'but I would still like to take you out again. I am working now until Sunday—can we go out then?'

'I can't promise,' said Tanya, 'I'm not sure what my arrangements are. I shall probably be going out with my sister, unless Juan claims her attention again.'

'I will come, just in case,' he said determinedly. 'I have enjoyed today very much.' He kissed her cheek briefly, shyly, '*Adiós*, Tanya, until Sunday.' With a roar of his engine he disappeared, leaving nothing but a cloud of dust behind.

Tanya had scarcely set foot in the house when Matilde said there was a phone call for her. It was Alejandro.

'Tanya,' he said abruptly, 'Matilde tells me you've been out all day with some boy. Who is he?'

It was a direct, no-beating-about-the-bush, question, and Tanya took offence at it. 'What business is it of yours?' she asked indignantly.

'I regard it very much as my business. You know no one here; I should hate you to get into the wrong company.'

That was rich, coming from him. If any man used a woman, it was Alejandro. 'You need have no fears in that respect,' she said tartly. 'He comes from a very good family.'

'What is his name?'

'Manuel.'

Alejandro snorted. 'There are dozens of Manuels in Tenerife. Did you find out his surname?'

'Yes, but I don't see that it's of any great importance. Why are you phoning me?' She heard his indrawn breath. He was angry with her for being evasive, but she did not care. He had no right at all to question her movements.

'I want you to come to Santa Cruz.'

It sounded like a mandate, and Tanya bridled. 'Just like that? You give the order and I run, is that what you're suggesting?'

'If that's how it sounded, I apologise,' he said stiffly. 'But it would be wrong of you to miss the *carnaval*, and I don't just mean the grand parade; I mean all of it — all the heats, all the dancing, all the excitement. I have an apartment in Santa Cruz; you can stay there.'

'No, thank you, I don't want to come.' Tanya deliberately hardened her voice.

'Your sister is at work, I presume?'

'Yes.'

'Then it is a ridiculous state of affairs,' he growled angrily. 'You cannot call sitting around there by yourself a holiday. Our *carnaval* is second only to Rio; it is the largest in Europe, and you should miss none of it.'

In truth Tanya thought it sounded pretty exciting, and it would be heaps better than amusing herself here, but to stay in Alejandro's apartment? It would be putting herself too much at risk.

'I am not using the apartment myself, Tanya, if that's what is worrying you.'

His astuteness surprised her.

'I would be with you during the day, naturally; most people take a week off work at this time of year. But I would return to my house in Orotava each evening. You'd have no need to feel threatened by my presence.'

'How thoughtful of you.' Tanya deliberately filled her tone with scorn.

Alejandro snorted his annoyance. '*Perdóneme*, I thought I was doing you a favour. If you don't want to enjoy the *carnaval*, then so be it. *Es tuya la perdida, no mia.*'

Tanya could just see in her mind's eye the arrogant

tilt to his head, the anger flashing in his eyes, but he deserved to be put down. Maybe it was because she had responded to his kiss that he thought she would jump at the opportunity. Maybe he did not know her as well as he thought!

'I didn't say I didn't want to come,' she said pointedly. In fact she thought it an excellent idea. Her holiday was beginning to pall, especially now Charlene had met Juan. He was all her sister could talk about. 'I'm merely suspicious about your motives.'

Another hiss of anger. 'You have made it very plain, *mi niña*, that you want nothing more to do with me. Our relationship will, I assure you, be strictly platonic — unless, of course, you change your mind.'

'I will never do that,' announced Tanya quickly. 'And in those circumstances I will be pleased to take you up on your offer, providing Charlene can stay with me if she gets any time off.'

'Naturally, she is very welcome — but —' and his tone hardened ' — not your male friend.'

Tanya was glad he could not see her smile. He actually sounded jealous, which was ridiculous when he had so many girlfriends. 'Manuel will not like it,' she said, trying to make her voice sound regretful, 'but yes, I will conform with your wishes.'

'Good.' It was a curt response. 'I will pick you up first thing in the morning. It was my plan to escort you there today, but — since you were otherwise occupied — that is now impossible; it is far too late. *Buenas noches*, Tanya.'

The line went dead before she could respond, and as she put the receiver down she wondered whether she was making a big mistake. He had said he would behave, but, knowing Alejandro, how could he? He was an extremely sensual man. Right from the start of their relationship they had been unable to keep their hands off each other; how could they spend a whole week together without succumbing?

Charlene was equally uneasy when Tanya told her about Alejandro's invitation. 'Goodness, Tan, that's the craziest thing I've ever heard; you're playing right into his hands. You know what the guy's like—he's only after your body.'

'He assured me that our relationship would be strictly platonic,' Tanya told her, 'And he won't be there at night; I'll have the apartment to myself.'

'And you believed him?' asked her sister incredulously. 'You want your head reading if you believe anything that man says. Have you forgotten already how he treated you? And how about all these other girls we've seen him out with?'

'There are only two.'

'And two's too many if he's setting his cap at you again. Oh, Tan, darling, don't make a fool of yourself a second time.' Charlene hugged her sister tightly. 'You can't kid me; I know you're still attracted to him—but he's not worth it, really he isn't. He's not serious about you; I don't think he could be serious about anyone. I don't think he even loved his wife as a man should—otherwise he wouldn't have started an affair with you.'

Tanya heaved a sigh. 'You're right, I know you're right, but it seems too good an opportunity to miss.'

Charlene grimaced wryly. 'It's all my fault that you're being neglected. Trust Carlos to go off sick at a time like this. And I don't actually blame you for wanting to go to Santa Cruz. The *carnaval* really is something. If you're so determined, all I can say is, be careful.'

'I will, I promise. I'm older and wiser now. I'm going into this with my eyes wide open.'

'So long as you don't leave your heart wide open. Tan, darling, I love you. I don't want you hurt again. And if I can scrounge a day or two off I'll be up there like a shot. You will ring me as soon as you know the address?'

*   *   *

Matilde, not knowing the underlying tension between Alejandro and Tanya, was pleased that she was going to see all of the *carnaval*, though she insisted that Tanya come back to her for the final days of her holiday.

Not unnaturally, Tanya slept little that night, tossing and turning in her normally comfortable bed, worrying, wondering what she was letting herself in for, hoping it was not a terrible mistake — like going to his party had been!

She must remember at all times to keep her distance, not to let herself get into any compromising situations. It would be all too easy to give in to the dictates of her body. Although her mind agreed with her that she hated Alejandro, her body thought otherwise; it never listened to anything it was told.

Alejandro turned up at eight, much earlier than Tanya had expected. Although he was casually dressed in beige trousers and shirt, he still looked devastating, and despite every good resolution she had made Tanya's heartbeats quickened. He was so good-looking, so erotic! How could any woman resist him?

Her case was packed and stood ready by the door. She had put on a pair of white cotton trousers and T-shirt, and Alejandro looked her up and down, slowly, thoughtfully, his eyes finally coming to rest on her face. 'You look tired, Tanya. I trust you didn't lie awake half the night worrying about whether you're doing the right thing?'

'I didn't sleep well, that's true,' she answered, wishing he couldn't read her so accurately, 'but only because I was hot.'

He didn't believe her; it was there in his eyes. 'It's much cooler in the north,' he announced, his lips quirking. 'You should have no difficulty sleeping there.'

Oh, but she would. How could she possibly settle in Alejandro's apartment, knowing that he had slept in the same bed, or, if not, in another room? His presence would be stamped indelibly all over it, and she wished too late that she had refused to go. Charlene was right; she was making a mistake, a giant one.

It was on the tip of her tongue to say that she had changed her mind when he said briskly, 'Right, if you're ready, we'll go.'

'What's the rush?' she asked. 'Matilde has some coffee on; wouldn't you like a cup?'

'Proscrastinating, Tanya?' The glint in his eye told her that he had guessed her thoughts.

She turned swiftly away. 'I was being polite, that's all.'

'Then we'll go.' He picked up her suitcase. '*Adiós*, Matilde.' He was outside the house in a matter of seconds, leaving Tanya to hurry after him. Her luggage was stowed in his boot. They both got in and he started the engine. Matilde waved them off.

It was as though she were going to another planet. Tanya felt that she was leaving everything that was comfortable and familiar behind her. She was going away with this man who had once been her lover, she was entrusting herself to him, believing him when he said there would be nothing sexual between them — and yet already it had started!

It was impossible to sit so close and not feel any reaction. It was faintly better because the car had an open top, but she was nevertheless still intensely aware of him — and if it was like this now what was it going to be like in a day or two's time?

She had thought he would drive south and pick up the motorway, making the journey to Santa Cruz so much quicker, but instead he headed in the opposite direction. 'Where are we going?' she asked with a faint frown.

'I thought I would take you to see my tomatoes. I still grow them, you know, the same as my father did.'

He was completely relaxed, a smile playing about his lips.

'I suppose there's no hurry,' she said, trying to hide her annoyance. 'Is there nothing going on today in Santa Cruz? I thought the whole idea was for me to see all the events.'

'And so it is,' he agreed, still smiling, 'But in the main they do not start until late afternoon, and some, like the election of the *reina del carnaval*, do not start until after nine. They go on very late, I'm afraid.'

Tanya took a deep, angry breath and sat up a little straighter, her eyes over-bright as she glared at him. 'You've tricked me, Alejandro. My days will be just as empty as before.'

'Oh, no, they won't,' he said confidently, 'Because you'll have me. We can do whatever you want to do — see the sights, swim, sunbathe, go walking. The world is your oyster, *mi cariño* — and you have to admit it will be much more fun than being on your own.'

'I hate you.' She looked straight ahead, her hands clenched tightly in her lap. 'You set this whole thing up. You let me believe that all of the events took part in the daytime.'

'Would you have come if I'd told you the truth?'

'Most definitely not,' she cried. 'In fact I insist that you turn around right now and take me back to Matilde's.'

'Not on your life, Tanya.' His foot went down on the accelerator as if to confirm his intention. 'We need to spend time together, and this was the only way I could think of arranging it. You're mine now, Tanya, for the next seven days, completely mine.'

She looked across at him, her eyes narrowed coldly. 'I've never belonged to you, and I never will.' Her heart was panicking. What a situation! She had never dreamt that he would do this to her. She tilted her chin. 'Once you go back to your house at night there'll be nothing to stop me leaving. I refuse to be your prisoner.'

Still he smiled infuriatingly. 'Not a prisoner, Tanya, never that, and who's to say I'll go home?'

Her blue eyes widened. 'But you promised.' Her heart thudded.

'Promises are made to be broken.' His voice had gone down to its gravelly depths, the way it always did when there were things on his mind other than prosaic conversation.

Tanya's mind darted this way and that, trying to think of a way she could get out of this situation. Nothing came immediately. She was trapped, whether she liked it or not. She had never thought he would do this to her; she had trusted him. But never again. If she got out of this unscathed — and she had every intention of doing just that — then she would make very certain that Alejandro played no further part in her life.

'You've gone very quiet, *amor mio*.'

'I am not your love,' she retorted furiously.

'You could be.'

'Along with Inocente and Beatriz?' Her eyes blazed as she looked at him.

'Beatriz is my *cuñada*, my sister-in-law.'

Again Tanya was stunned. She really was making quite a fool of herself. Her voice was little more than a whisper when she said, 'Why didn't you tell me?'

'Because I thought Matilde would have said.'

Tanya shook her head. 'She did introduce us, but you know how quickly she speaks. I caught the name Vázquez, but that was all.'

'So you assumed she was my wife, and then later, when I knocked that little theory on the head, you thought she was my mistress? What an opinion you have of me.'

'I'm sorry, Alejandro.'

'*Sorry*?' It was his turn to be angry. 'I seem to be

getting the blame for all sorts of things I haven't done, and I'm not sure that I like it.'

Tanya wanted to tell him that if he hadn't done the dirty on her in the first place she would never have jumped to such conclusions, but he wouldn't listen, she knew, not in the mood he was in at this moment, and she could hardly blame him. And there was still Inocente, who was apparently his current girlfriend, and if that was the case why was he insisting on spending time with her, Tanya? It was a whole mixed-up situation.

'Have you nothing more to say for yourself?' Gone were the low, sensual tones, replaced by a cold hardness that made Tanya squirm.

'It was a legitimate mistake, one anyone could have made,' she returned defensively. 'And you haven't told me about Inocente; what does she mean to you?'

'Inocente is my friend.'

'Your *friend*?' asked Tanya, her tone derisive. 'She looks far more than that to me. The girl's in love with you.'

'We are close, yes,' he admitted.

More than close, thought Tanya. Lovers might be a more accurate description.

'You are jealous of Inocente?'

Tanya tossed him a swift, sceptical glance. 'That's the very last thing I'd feel. You're welcome to her; you're welcome to as many girls as you like. Just don't try and add me to your list.'

His hands clenched the wheel suddenly, knuckles white, and Tanya guessed she had struck a raw nerve. He hated to think that he had once had her in the palm of his hand and then lost her; he hated the thought that she might never really have had any deep affection for him. He needed to try and prove himself. He had a massive male ego, and she had bruised it.

Within half an hour they had reached his tomato *finca*, and Tanya was extremely impressed. There were acres and acres of tomato plants growing in serried ranks, much bigger and thicker than any she had seen in England. They were supported by twigs and taller than a person, and women were between the rows, picking the tomatoes, putting them into baskets, in which they would eventually be transferred to the packing plant.

'What surprises me,' said Tanya, 'is that the Canary tomatoes we have in England are very small, and yet I've seen no small ones here. Why is that? Are there different sorts?'

'No, they're all the same,' he said, shaking his head. 'It's just that the English specify small tomatoes. You will see later how they're graded on conveyors. Such places as Holland and Belgium, Mexico, the USA, they all want big ones.'

'They're certainly much tastier,' agreed Tanya.

Some of the tomatoes, growing on higher ground, were sheltered from the strong winds that sometimes blew on the island by walls of strong nylon sheeting stretched between posts.

They did not stay long; the tension between them was too great. It was a brief, whistle-stop tour, and then they were on their way again. The road through the mountains climbed higher and higher, and Tanya caught occasional glimpses of Teide in the distance, snow-peaked and dramatic against an unbelievably deep blue sky. They passed through a village where purple and red bougainvillaea made a brilliant splash of colour against the white walls of the houses.

He drove a little too quickly round dangerous hairpin bends, the wind blew through her hair, and the higher they climbed the colder it became, and the silence between them was tangible. Stopping to look at his tomatoes being grown had done nothing to lessen the tension.

When they reached the road that took them past Mount Teide he finally spoke. 'Do you want to stop and take a closer look? Take a ride in the cable car, maybe?'

Tanya shook her head. 'I went up with Charlene, but I could do with a jumper out of my case.' If she had known when they set off that he was going to bring her this way she would have been prepared. There was frozen snow on the lava either side of the road, frozen snow on the shrubs and plants. She knew it was frozen because she and Charlene had tried to make snowballs. It amazed her that the sun didn't melt it more quickly; she had learned that it took months for it to disappear off the top of the mountain.

Alejandro stopped the car and opened the boot, waiting while she unsnapped her case and took out a thick jumper. He shrugged into a jacket himself, and then they were on their way again. Neither spoke.

They dropped slowly down out of the mountains, through town after town, until finally, thankfully, they reached the outskirts of the capital.

'Where is your apartment?' Tanya spoke without thinking, and it was as though her voice had cracked the silence, for Alejandro looked at her and faintly smiled. 'Not far now.'

Tanya had not been to Santa Cruz before and found it was not quite what she had expected. She had always thought that all capitals were beautiful, but this one wasn't. And as if knowing what she was thinking, Alejandro said, 'It might not have great looks, but it has great people. It's nicknamed "Capital de la Amabilidad", the Capital of Kindness. The Santacruceros are a warm, friendly people, as you'll find out.'

If I stay long enough, thought Tanya.

His apartment was at the top of a high-rise block, not very far from the commercial centre. A high-speed lift took them up, and once inside Tanya was staggered by its opulence. She had expected a tiny bachelor apartment, furnished with only the essentials for infrequent visits; instead it was a veritable home from home. It wanted for nothing; it was as luxurious as his house in Orotava.

'Do you stay here often?' she asked. Perhaps he used it as his love-nest, entertained his lady-friends here.

'I used to, when Juanita was alive,' he told her. 'She loved it here. I'm afraid I only stay now when business dictates.'

Instantly Tanya felt ashamed of her traitorous thoughts and was glad she had not voiced them aloud.

'If you're hungry there's plenty of food in the kitchen,' he said.

Tanya frowned. 'Does that mean you're leaving?'

'Isn't it what you want?' His tone was clipped, his face expressionless.

'Of course not. You can't bring me to a strange place and then just dump me. I might as well have stayed where I was. Take me back if you're not happy with the situation.'

'I don't want to do that, Tanya, and you know it.'

Their eyes met and warred for several long, painful seconds, then he heaved a sigh and pulled her into his arms. 'Oh, Tanya *mio*, why do we argue like this?'

She did not answer; she simply allowed the warmth of him to flood into her, allowed feelings to rise, and marvelled that she could feel like this when seconds earlier she had wished herself a million miles away.

'It is not what I want at all,' he murmured in her ear. 'I want this to be an enjoyable week for you, for us, I want us to get to know one another all over again — and, of course, I also want you to enjoy our *carnaval*.' He said the word proudly. This annual event meant a lot to him, as it did to most Tinerfeños.

But that was a secondary consideration, she realised now. His main aim was for them to resume their relationship of nine years ago. She ought to have known, ought to have guessed what he had in mind. Or perhaps she had known, and that was why she had agreed to come. Perhaps deep down she *wanted* to carry on where they had left off. Didn't her body still crave his? Wasn't it still as wonderful between them?

'Tanya?' He lifted her chin, compelling her to look at him, and desire flared within her.

'I want to enjoy it too,' she whispered.

CHAPTER SIX

TANYA woke the next morning to rain and grey skies, and she could not believe it. This was the first time since she had been out here that she had seen rain. Some days had been cloudy, yes, but they had always cleared quickly, leaving blue skies behind. Now the sky looked as though it would remain like this for the rest of the day, and it was much cooler too than in the south, suggesting it would be sensible to wear sweater and trousers, not suntop and shorts.

She yawned and stretched and looked around the bedroom. The furniture here was not quite so overpowering as in Matilde's house. It still had a fairly heavy look to it, but it was in a pine shade rather than dark oak, and the rugs at the side of the bed were in a sea-green and cream weave which matched the bedspread.

It was the largest of the three bedrooms, and Alejandro had insisted that she take it. She guessed it was the one that he and Juanita had shared, and no doubt it held too many memories for him ever to use it again. But it hadn't helped her, sleeping in the same bed as he had, and she had spent half the night wishing he were there beside her.

Through the window she could see clouds boiling around the peaks of the Anaga mountains, stormy and dramatic, a very stirring background to the city.

Yesterday had turned out all right after all. She had fixed them a salad after they had finally made their peace, and then they had walked around Santa Cruz. She had told him about Manuel, who he really was, assuring him that there was nothing between them, and he had accepted her word, though she had seen for a moment his anger when she brought up the boy's name.

They spent some time standing on the promenade along the outer sea walls, watching the big ships come and go. 'Santa Cruz is a major port as well as an administrative and commercial centre,' Alejandro told her.

However, it was the preparations for the *carnaval* that impressed her most. There was a huge stage and backdrop in the main square, the Plaza de España. 'This is where all the judging takes place,' Alejandro informed her, 'where the groups of dancers and singers perform, where the heats for the carnival queen, both children and adults, are held, and where the grand final for the *reina del carnaval* is played out to its conclusive and glorious moments,' He was very enthusiastic about it, and Tanya could not help feeling some excitement too.

Later, much later, they found a quiet little restaurant, and then he took her back to the apartment. Half expecting him to say that he was going to stay the night, Tanya was surprised when, after a disappointing kiss on her brow, he announced his intention of leaving.

'It is best,' he said. 'You are too beautiful; you arouse in me great desire. If I do not go now, *mi cariño*, I will be unable to go at all.'

Tanya felt great excitement at the thought of him spending the night in her bed, but she knew it would be insanity, and something she would deeply regret later. She must never forget that it would mean nothing to him. 'And you would be breaking your promise,' she pointed out.

'Indeed, but I will think of you, alone here in your bed. Perhaps you will think of me a little too?'

'Oh, I expect I shall think of you,' she said, 'But not in exactly the same way. I shall be thinking how relieved I am that you've gone home. And I've no doubt Inocente would be relieved too, if she knew of the situation.' It helped her to bring in the other girl's name, helped her remember what a swine he was. It was all too easy to forget; he could be so charming, so attentive; he could make her feel that she meant everything to him.

The last few hours of peace might never have been. He drew in a harsh, angry breath, mentally withdrawing from her, his eyes a hard core of jet. 'I thought I had convinced you that Inocente is no more than a good friend. It seems I was mistaken.'

'No, you didn't convince me,' retorted Tanya. 'You can say what you like, I know only what my eyes tell me, and when she finds out that you've installed me here I guess she'll be one very angry lady. Unless you don't tell her.'

'Of course I shall tell her,' he said. 'I have nothing to hide. You are grossly mistaken in thinking that she would be hurt. She understands what my relationship with you is.'

Tanya looked at him, her head on one side. 'Really? Then she knows more than me. What did you tell her, that *we're* just good friends as well? I should be interested to hear what you consider our relationship is.'

'It doesn't matter what I told her,' he answered sharply. 'What is of importance, is why are you being particularly difficult.'

'Am I?' Tanya feigned innocence. 'I hadn't realised.'

'*Maldito sea*, Tanya, you know very well you are. Why do you keep harping on about Inocente? Why cannot we forget her, enjoy ourselves, recapture some of our past magic?'

Past magic? Yes, it had been that all right, until she had seen his father's letter about Juanita and the nightmare had begun. She would never forget that moment, or the way Alejandro had left England without so much as a word. How could they ever get back on to any sort of footing after that? 'It is not possible,' she said faintly.

'Not possible because you are being stubborn,' he growled, gripping her shoulders so hard that he hurt. 'If you relaxed and let go a little you would see that there is still a lot of pleasure to be had.'

'Maybe I don't want pleasure of that sort.' She eyed him stonily, bravely.

'Why?' he snarled, and then, as a sudden thought struck him, 'Is it because of Peter? Do you have some sort of hang-up where he is concerned? Do you feel it would be disloyal to let yourself get close to another man?'

'Of course not,' Tanya cried, 'but you're living under a delusion. You and I were never that close; there is nothing to recapture.'

'Pardon me.' His eyes grew steely. 'I thought there was.' And as if to add emphasis to his words he slid his hands down to her bottom and pulled her hard against him.

It was impossible to stop the flood of feelings, especially when he lowered his head and touched his lips to hers. It was like putting a match to a dry piece of paper — she ignited immediately. 'Actually, the magic *is* still there,' he muttered against her mouth. 'All it needs is a little encouragement.'

Tanya could not answer him. Her lips were parted against his, her whole body throbbing, and every thought of denying or rejecting him had fled. It took no more than a touch to have her melt in his arms, the briefest brush of his lips, the feel of his hard body against hers.

However much hatred she might feel, there was no denying the strong physical chemistry that bonded them together, or at least bonded her to him. Alejandro had no sense of loyalty. He had played around with her even though he had another girl back home, and now he was doing the very same thing,

pushing Inocente into the background while he
renewed his affair with her. Probably, once she had
gone back to England, he would marry Inocente — that
seemed to be the way he worked.

Yet even while her mind admitted all this her body
still craved his. She hadn't the strength to reject him.
Her mouth moved against his and her hands slid
upwards to cradle his head. She put her all into the
kiss, drinking eagerly from his mouth, feeling her
whole body pulse and race and grow warm.

It was Alejandro who called a halt, who finally,
gently, put her from him. There was a question in his
eyes. 'Unless you want me to stay the night?'

Yes, yes, yes, her heart clamoured. No, no, no,
insisted her mind. She shook her head, not trusting
herself to speak.

'Then I'll leave now, while I still have the will-power.
But I'll be round early tomorrow.' He cupped her face
between strong brown hands. 'You are still as lovely as
I remember, still my beautiful Tanya. Hell, I missed
you. I wish. . .' He broke off suddenly. '*Buenas
noches, amor mio*; miss me a little bit.'

He had gone then, leaving Tanya wondering what he
had been going to say. What did he wish? Was it
something to do with their breaking up? Had he been
about to offer explanations? Whatever, she wouldn't
have accepted them. There was no possible reason he
could give for leaving her, other than he thought it
time to put an end to their relationship.

Today she would be strong, she decided the next
morning as she stood beneath the refreshing jets of the
shower; today she would not let him kiss her. It spelled
disaster; it fuelled the very real desire that, much to
her disgust, still lay buried deep inside her.

He had not said exactly what time he would come.
'Early' to Tanya meant perhaps ten or eleven or even
early afternoon, certainly not before nine, which was
when he came hammering on the door.

Inevitably her heartbeats quickened, and she checked her appearance in the mirror by the door before opening it. Her smile of welcome faded somewhat when she saw that Alejandro was accompanied by a small boy.

'We have company today,' he said as he moved inside. 'Tanya, this is my son, Manolo. Manolo, *esta es la señora de quien hablé.*'

Very correctly the boy held out his hand and Tanya took it, all the time thinking, Alejandro's *son*! Alejandro had a son! She was shocked to the very core. 'It is good to meet you, Manolo,' she said, her tone faint.

The boy did not speak, merely looking at her shyly. She judged him to be about seven, dark-haired, slim and with big brown eyes like his father's. Other than that he looked nothing like him. Tanya guessed that the boy took after his mother, with his fine straight nose and slightly pointed chin.

'The children's *carnaval* queen gala is being held this afternoon and Manolo wants to see it,' Alejandro informed her. 'His favourite cousin has entered; isn't that right, Manolo?'

The boy frowned. '*No comprendo*, Papá.'

Tanya expected Alejandro to speak to his son in his native language; instead he said patiently in much slower English, 'You want to see Doña?'

Manolo smiled widely, his even white teeth shining. '*Sí*, Papá, *sí. Espero que ella gane.*'

Alejandro frowned. 'Manolo, please speak in English. Tanya will not understand what you are saying.'

'I am sorry, Papá,' said the boy at once, and hesitatingly to Tanya, 'I did not know you could not speak my language.'

'It's all right,' she said with a careful smile, admiring the fact that he could speak English so well. He made her feel very inadequate.

'Papá, *puede* — I mean, can I have a look around?'

'Of course,' Alejandro said, 'except in the room Tanya is using; it is the big bedroom. You must not go in there; it would be very rude.'

'OK, Papá.' And he skipped off happily.

'I trust you slept well.' Alejandro looked at Tanya and smiled warmly.

She nodded. 'Very well, thank you. Why didn't you tell me you had a son?'

He shrugged. 'The need never arose, and as a matter of fact I don't know whether you have any children either. We seem not to have had any deep, meaningful conversations. Perhaps it is time.'

'No, I haven't any children, and no, I don't want any in-depth talks,' answered Tanya tartly.

'You're angry with me for not telling you about Manolo?'

'Not really; it has nothing to do with me, has it? It's a surprise, though, I must admit.' More than a surprise, a shock of the highest order.

'You wish I hadn't brought him today?'

'Heavens, no!' exclaimed Tanya at once. 'He's — he's very welcome. It will be nice to have — other company.'

'You mean a chaperon?' His brows rose and he looked at her quizzically, but there was a quirk to his lips, and Tanya knew that he had been thinking the same thing.

'Things do seem to get a bit tense between us,' she agreed. 'It might help having him with us. What time does the judging start?'

'Not until four. I thought we might take Manolo to the beach.'

Tanya nodded. Amazingly the rain, which had looked set in for the whole day, had cleared, and although the skies weren't particularly clear the sun shone at this moment. 'An excellent idea.' A beach meant crowds, no chance of their getting close. Yes, it was a superb suggestion.

'I guess you haven't done much swimming since you've been here.'

Tanya confessed that she hadn't. 'But it's my own choice. A boy pushed me in a lake when I was little, and I've been terrified of water since. Charlene made me learn to swim, but I'm not very good and I don't enjoy it.'

'That's a pity.' Alejandro frowned. 'Manolo swims like a fish; I taught him myself at an extremely early age. But never mind; today you need not be afraid. I will personally keep my eye on you.'

Tanya was not sure whether she liked the reassurance. She would much prefer to sunbathe while Alejandro and his son enjoyed the water.

'Have you eaten?' he asked next.

'I've had a bread roll and some marmalade,' she said, 'and there's still some coffee in the pot if you'd like one.'

By this time Manolo had finished his tour of the apartment and was bouncing up and down on the white leather settee. 'I think we should go,' said Alejandro, 'before I have no furniture left. We'll show Manolo the ships first. They are a passion of his. It's his ambition to join the Navy when he grows up. He wants to be an admiral. Or he might be an explorer like Christopher Columbus,' he added with a laugh. 'He has big ideas for so small a boy.'

It was about twelve by the time they reached Las Teresitas, and Tanya could not believe what she saw. Tenerife being a volcanic island, almost all of its beaches were black sand, at least the ones she had seen. Here it was white.

'Am I seeing things?' she asked Alejandro.

He spread his hands expansively. 'The biggest man-made beach in the world. Four million sacks of sand were shipped here from the Spanish Sahara.'

'I'm impressed,' said Tanya.

'It's a favourite bathing spot for all Santacruceros,'

he told her. It was dotted with palms and an occasional stand that sold cold drinks, et cetera. There was parking along the road for hundreds of cars, and Manolo was out like a flash and down on to the sand. Alejandro smiled fondly. 'Let's join him.'

Manolo was already pulling off his shirt and trousers, anxious to get in the water, and Alejandro followed suit. In fact they seemed to be having a race, and Tanya watched them, smiling, thinking what a wonderful relationship they had.

They both had their swimming-trunks on underneath, and the moment they were ready they dashed towards the sea. The skies had cleared altogether now, and the water was a wonderful blue-green. Father and son played together like porpoises.

Tanya spread her towel and stripped off her own sweater and cotton trousers. She too had put on her bikini before coming out, and now she smoothed in sun-cream before lying back to enjoy the warmth of the sun. It did not feel quite so hot as in the south, but it was hot enough. She closed her eyes and relaxed, listening to the sound of youths shouting, children squealing, mothers consoling, and then she felt cold water dripping on to her stomach.

When she opened her eyes both Alejandro and Manolo were standing over her, laughing, shaking their wet hands over her body. 'We've come to get you,' said Alejandro.

'Yes,' said the boy.

'We refuse to let you lie here.'

'We want you to join us.'

'Do I have any choice?' asked Tanya, sitting up.

'None at all,' answered Alejandro.

'Is the water cold?'

'Not once you're used to it.' He held out his hands and she took them, allowing him to pull her to her feet. Contact, even something as innocent as this, triggered a sudden warmth through her body, but she knew she had to be careful because of Manolo. What his father had told him about her, she was not sure, but it could be nothing more than that they had met in England, certainly not that he was after some sort of affair with her now.

Tanya walked reluctantly with them towards the ocean which had looked so beautiful from her position on the sand but which now looked positively menacing. There was so much of it, and it was so deep and so strong, and she was so afraid.

Sensing her hesitation, Alejandro took her hand. 'I'll be with you every inch of the way.' And to his son, 'Tanya does not swim very well; we must look after her.' So Manolo took her other hand, and between them they led her into the water.

It was cold, icy cold, and when they were a few feet out Alejandro suggested she dip herself completely into the water. 'The quicker you do it, the better it will be.' And because she did not want to make a fool of herself, Tanya obeyed. It took her breath away at first, but then she began to discover that it wasn't so cold after all.

They waded out another couple of yards until it was up to her breasts. 'Now let's see what you can do,' said Alejandro.

'I can't do anything.' Tanya was suddenly terrified of taking her feet off the bottom. 'I'm scared. I can't do it, Alejandro. I want to go back.'

But he would hear none of it. 'Try floating. I'll put my hand under your back; you have nothing to fear.' And more softly, 'Trust me, *mi cariño*.'

His hand was solid and comforting behind her, and gradually she allowed herself to fall backwards, her feet coming up, until finally she was floating on the surface of the water, Alejandro's hand still beneath her.

'Relax,' he murmured mesmerically. 'Close your eyes and think of something nice.' And because she knew he was there, because she knew he would let nothing happen to her, Tanya did so, and when Alejandro moved his hand away she remained floating, and she marvelled that she was doing it without feeling any fear. That was the main thing, not her achievement. Alejandro was giving her confidence.

Manolo too floated at her side, and when she opened her eyes and looked at him he grinned. 'It is easy, yes?'

Within half an hour Tanya found herself actually swimming and enjoying it — for the first time in her life she was enjoying it. Alejandro never moved away from her; he swam at her side, or stood and watched, and always he was there at the ready in case she should panic, always offering her words of encouragement.

Manolo had joined a group of boys his own age, and she and Alejandro were alone. They were floating again now, side by side, and he said quietly, 'Tanya, you are driving me crazy, do you know that? You are as irresistible to me now as you were nine years ago.'

She wished he hadn't said that, because nine years ago he had left England without contacting her again. In less than a week after their argument he had gone. She couldn't have been that irresistible! 'You have a smooth tongue, Alejandro.'

'You do not believe me?'

'Once I would have believed you, but not any longer. Now I suspect you say the same sort of thing to every girl.'

He gave a snort of anger and rolled off his back to tread water at her side. 'That was uncalled for.'

'Was it?' she asked, looking into the angry dark depths of his eyes. 'Not from this side of the fence. In any case, a lot's happened since then. I'm not quite the gullible young girl I was. We had a good time while it lasted, but it's over, forgotten, and that's how I'd like it to remain.'

'I'm not getting through to you, am I, Tanya?'

'No.' She rolled off her back too and began to swim

towards the shore, and this time she did not need him to give her confidence; she was swimming automatically, capably — and she amazed herself.

He easily caught her up. 'Haven't I made myself clear that I'd like to begin all over again?'

Tanya's feet touched the bottom. 'Perfectly, but I don't happen to feel the same way.'

'Because there's someone else in your life?'

She started to wade out of the water. 'No.'

'Then why?' He was walking with her, looking at her, trying to make her see his point of view.

'Let's say that when I walked out of your hotel room all those years ago it was a decision I've never regretted. I've never wished to undo it, to resume a relationship with you. It didn't work then; it wouldn't work now.' Hell, why was she lying, why did she consistently push him away from her? The answer was simple — she did not trust him.

'It could work, Tanya.'

'No.' She shook her head determinedly. 'I refuse to even give it a try. You're wasting your time.'

'Papá, Papá, wait for me.' Manolo had spotted his father leaving.

Alejandro turned but Tanya carried on, and when they joined her she was lying face down on her towel.

'I think Tanya is tired,' said Manolo.

'I think so too,' said Alejandro.

'I would like a drink, Papá.'

'Then we will go and get you one.'

Silence reigned as they moved away, and Tanya squinted at them through half-closed eyes. Manolo was trying to match his stride to his father's, his head tilted at exactly the same angle, his hands clasped similarly behind his back. He clearly adored his father and, what was more important, was extremely well-behaved.

When they returned she was still lying in the same position, but sat up instantly when Manolo said, 'Wake up, Tanya; we have a Coke for you.'

'Thank you.' She took the can from the boy and they both sat down on their towels beside her, and there was silence as they all drank thirstily through their straws. Manolo was the first to finish, noisily, happily. 'Can we swim again now?'

'I'll stay here with Tanya,' said Alejandro. 'You go and play with your new friends. Don't go out too far.'

'No, Papá.'

The boy ran off happily enough, and Tanya said, 'He's a nice boy, well-behaved and well-adjusted. You've done a good job on him.'

'It was no hardship,' he said with a shrug of his wide shoulders. 'We were always close, even before Juanita died.'

'Was she ill long?' asked Tanya, recalling Peter's lengthy period of poor health.

'No, no, it was an accident. A hit-and-run affair. They never caught the person who did it.' A shadow chased across his face, and Tanya could see his mind going back to that painful time.

'I'm so sorry.' Unthinkingly she laid her hand on his arm.

He put his much bigger hand over hers. 'Manolo was just over two at the time. The poor little fellow could not understand what had happened. He needed me then and he's clung to me ever since.'

Which made him just turned eight now, not seven as she had thought. Which meant——

Alejandro's voice cut into her thoughts. 'It was a long time ago, Tanya.' He had evidently mistaken her sudden tension for sympathy over his loss.

Her eyes flashed. 'I was actually thinking that if Manolo is eight you didn't waste much time in marrying Juanita.' Her tone was sharply critical, and she snatched her hand away from beneath his.

'You were the one who put an end to our relationship, Tanya,' he pointed out coldly.

Was that what he really thought? Hadn't it occurred

to him that if he'd come after her she would have said how much she loved him, admitted she had been wrong not to believe his declaration that he did not love Juanita? Now that she had met Manolo she knew that she had been right. 'I'm glad that I did,' she spat savagely. 'If I wasn't sure before that I had done the right thing, I am now.'

'You had doubts?' he asked sharply.

Tanya shrugged. 'Only in my weaker moments.'

'And were there many of those?' His eyes were intent upon hers.

'For the first few days, that's all,' she cried. 'After that I put you right out of my mind.'

Her harsh words fuelled Alejandro's anger and he jerked himself furiously to his feet. 'I am wasting my time. I will get my son and take him to see the *eleccion de la reina infantil*. You can please yourself whether you come or not.'

CHAPTER SEVEN

TANYA went to the election of the juvenile queen, but only because Manolo insisted. When she declared, after they had eaten their lunch in a side-street restaurant, that she was going back to the apartment he caught her hand anxiously. 'No, no, Tanya, you must come with us. Papá, tell her; make her come.' He seemed to have taken an instant liking to her, and actually the feeling was mutual. Tanya was fond of him too.

Banks of seats were erected in the square for the audience, and Manolo sat between her and Alejandro. They looked like an average happy family, thought Tanya; how deceptive appearances could be. Manolo was disappointed when his cousin did not win, although slightly appeased when she was selected as one of the queen's entourage.

On their drive back to the apartment the boy went to sleep, and once they got there Alejandro said he was taking his son home.

'Do you usually stay here?' asked Tanya.

Alejandro nodded.

'I'm sorry.' But if he thought she would suggest they did so now he was mistaken. The more time they spent together the less easy it was to pretend indifference.

Once indoors she sat down on the white leather couch and pondered over her discovery that Alejandro and Juanita had got married almost immediately he came home from England. It was a hard fact to take in. And twelve months later—probably less than that, depending on when his birthday was—Manolo had been born!

It proved beyond any shadow of doubt that she,

Tanya, had meant nothing to him. He had needed female company while he was in England and she had proved the perfect companion, giving him her all. He must have thought his luck was in. And then the instant things had gone a little wrong between them he had turned tail and fled, without giving her another thought!

She wished now that she had never let him cajole her into coming here to Santa Cruz. Everything was worse than she had imagined. She got up and paced the room, looked out through the window at the receding shape of the mountains, at the pinpoints of light beginning to appear in the buildings climbing their slopes, looked down at the cars in the street below, turned and looked at the room with its white tiled floor and pine furniture and the glossy green leaves of exotic plants which added to its still coolness.

She shivered and suddenly thought longingly of England with its carpeted floors and central heating or cosy coal fires. She wanted to go back to her house where she felt safe and secure; she did not want to stay here where Alejandro unsettled her.

The telephone rang, and it startled her in the silence of the room. Alejandro! Her heart pattered as she picked it up. 'Hello?'

But it was her sister, ringing to ask where she had been. 'I was going to come and see you,' she said accusingly.

Tanya explained about their day out, and the discovery of Alejandro's son, and had only just set the phone down when it rang again. This time it *was* Alejandro. 'Get yourself ready,' he told her. 'We're having supper out.'

Although she was hungry Tanya said sharply, 'Oh, no, we're not. Besides, it's much too far for you to keep travelling backwards and forwards from Orotava.'

'That's my problem, not yours,' he told her gruffly. 'I'll be there in half an hour.'

The phone went dead before she could speak again, and Tanya was left with no choice. He had sounded as though he was only making the offer because he thought it was the right thing to do. He needn't have bothered; she would have much preferred to spend the evening alone.

No, that wasn't strictly true; she did not want to be alone, but her own company would certainly be better than Alejandro's. They had nothing in common any more, except perhaps an unwanted animal attraction. Maybe this was what they'd had all along. Maybe she had never loved him. Maybe she had mistaken physical pleasure for love. He was the only man who had ever stimulated her to the extreme in this way.

Peter's lovemaking had been gentle and certainly less than innovative, but she had been happy and satisfied because he had been loving in other ways too, her friend as well as her lover, her right arm when she had needed him, always obliging, always happy and generous and thoughtful.

Alejandro had some of these traits too, but it had been the physical side of their relationship that had been dominant, and, looking back, she could see that she had put this before everything else. She had hungered for his body but not his soul and his mind — and those feelings were still there, unfortunately.

He turned up in thirty minutes exactly, and Tanya was waiting. She was given a thorough appraisal, starting at the tip of her pink-painted toenails, at her strappy white sandals, right up the slender length of her legs to the curve of her hips and the swell of her breasts beneath her pink linen dress, finally coming to rest on her face, their eyes meeting, but his giving nothing away.

Tanya felt uncomfortably warm, and she expected some comment, a compliment perhaps, but all he said was, 'Good, you're ready. Let's go.'

With a mental shrug she slipped into her white

jacket, picked up her bag, and followed him out to the lift. There was still an atmosphere between them, and she wished he had not suggested they go out. It was going to be a tense, difficult evening.

They sat in silence in his Mercedes, the soft cover pulled over on this cool February evening, and instead of taking her to a restaurant in Santa Cruz, as she had expected, he drove along the La Cuesta highway to the university town of La Laguna. It was only a matter of eight kilometres, and once there he pulled up outside a big house in one of the narrow streets in the old part of the town. Tanya looked at him in surprise.

'Where are we?'

'At my brother's.'

'But——'

'It is all right; you've been invited.'

Tanya shook her head, feeling a little bemused. She had no wish to meet any members of his family. Why had he invited her? What had he said? How about Inocente—where did she fit into all of this? Wasn't she Alejandro's girlfriend? Oughtn't she to have been asked instead?

He pushed open a huge, carved wooden door and they stepped into a plant-filled patio along similar lines to his own. It amazed Tanya that there was this oasis of green just the other side of an innocent-looking wall. It must be, she thought, that all the older houses had these private, beautiful courtyards.

Immediately a side-door opened, and to Tanya's surprise Beatriz came forward to greet them. 'Alejandro, welcome.' They embraced and kissed warmly, as they had at the airport when Tanya had mistaken her for his wife. 'And Tanya, I am so glad you have at last come.' She kissed Tanya on each cheek. 'I keep asking Alejandro to bring you; he say you are always doing something else. Come inside and meet my husband. He is looking forward to seeing you.'

Alejandro's brother looked nothing like him, much shorter and with a paunch, his dark hair already receding even though he was a few years younger. 'Crisógono, meet Tanya. Tanya, my husband,' introduced Beatriz.

'So you are the mysterious Tanya.' Crisógono gave her a warm, welcoming smile and a bear-like hug. 'We heard about you when Alejandro came back from his time spent in England and couldn't believe it when he said he'd met you again recently.' His English was as perfect as Alejandro's and Tanya remembered Beatriz saying that her husband too had been to England.

Alejandro had told his family about her all those years ago! Tanya was shocked, and wondered exactly what he had said—especially since Juanita had been waiting at home for him. He could not have told them that they'd had a sizzling affair; he must have hinted that she was someone he'd met—a platonic friend, no more. On the other hand, he had declared that he'd written to Juanita, telling the girl about her. Perhaps they did know. Perhaps everyone knew. Perhaps they thought that they might get back together again now that he was a widower. Heavens, it was so embarrassing.

'It's very kind of you to invite me,' she said with a faint smile. 'You must forgive me if I seem confused. Alejandro did not tell me we were coming here.'

'Alejandro!' exclaimed his sister-in-law at once. 'You are very naughty.'

'I thought it would be a nice surprise,' he insisted, smiling at Beatriz, looking at Tanya speculatively.

She did not respond. She was, in fact, not sure how to behave. She had no idea what sort of a relationship she was supposed to be having with Alejandro.

'You are very welcome,' announced Crisógono. 'Come and sit down; I will pour you a drink.'

They were in a large room filled to overflowing with large pieces of furniture and the inevitable pot plants, and Tanya chose a deep, comfortable armchair. Alejandro lowered himself into the chair next to her, separated only by a small, square, black-carved table with a beautiful figurine of the madonna standing on it.

Tanya wished he had chosen to sit somewhere else. It made them seem like a couple, which they were most definitely not.

Crisógono handed her a glass with just a drop of wine in the bottom which he proudly announced was from his own vineyard. 'Taste it and tell me what you think.'

Tanya sipped the golden liquid and tried not to grimace when she found it too sweet, like the one Matilde usually gave her. Perhaps all the local wines were sweet. But Crisógono, who had been watching her closely, said at once, 'You do not like it? Drink no more; I have another.' Within a matter of seconds her glass was replaced. 'Smell the bouquet,' he said proudly. 'Savour it. You will like this one, I am sure.'

Tanya smiled. He was being very dramatic. But when she tasted the wine it was much more to her taste, and she nodded enthusiastically. 'Yes, I like this one, thank you.' She held out her glass so that he could fill it.

'And you, Alejandro, my brother, what will you have to drink — your usual whisky?'

Alejandro inclined his head.

'My brother does not like my wine,' Crisógono told Tanya, shaking his head sadly. 'He has far more sophisticated tastes.'

It was true, thought Tanya. Crisógono was very much more down to earth than Alejandro, despite the fact that they were both farmers — in different ways; both worked the land, and in fact the younger man's produce went through quite a sophisticated process once the grapes were picked, whereas Alejandro's tomatoes were simply picked and sold. It was an odd parallel.

'Of course he has,' said Beatriz, 'when you consider the company he keeps.'

Tanya frowned.

'He has not told you of his other interest?' asked Beatriz.

She shook her head. 'No.'

'Alejandro, shame on you. Have you not taken her out on your yacht?'

'No, I haven't, Beatriz,' answered Alejandro sharply. 'We do not have the close relationship you are insinuating. Tanya is someone I once knew very briefly, that is all.'

'What do you mean "knew briefly"? asked his sister-in-law, equally sharply. 'Were you not lovers in England?'

'That was a long time ago,' answered Alejandro calmly. 'We are now both older and wiser. We are not so close.'

Tanya felt her cheeks colouring—so he *had* told them! She pasted a brilliant smile to her lips and pretended she was not disturbed by this discussion about their relationship. 'What is this, Alejandro, about a yacht? Goodness, how could you keep something so exciting to yourself?'

He looked at her then, smiling slowly. 'There is no mystery; it is a business interest. I charter it—to the rich and famous, complete with crew, though sometimes I captain it myself; it all depends. *Zafra*—that is the tomato season—is from late October to the end of April. The rest of the year there is not much to do except prepare the ground for the following year's crop. It is a sideline, that's all.'

'And an extremely profitable one,' added Crisógono.

'But not so satisfying as growing tomatoes, Cris,' pointed out Alejandro. 'It is fun, yes, but there is no end-product. It is like one big holiday, and after a while it becomes tedious.'

He said it so matter-of-factly that Tanya laughed out loud. 'If that's tedium, what is my job?'

'What do you do?' asked Beatriz with interest

'I'm a PA.' And when the woman frowned, 'I'm sorry, I'm a personal assistant — to the managing director of a computer software company.'

'That sounds very important,' said the other woman.

'My boss depends on me a lot, I suppose,' confessed Tanya.

'And he has let you come away on a month's holiday?'

Tanya smiled. 'He owes it me. I haven't taken my full quota of holidays for the last few years.' Ever since Peter died, in fact. There seemed no point when she had no one to go away with.

'How much longer have you left?'

'Just under two weeks.'

'Enough time to see our *carnaval*,' concluded Beatriz happily. 'I am so glad Alejandro persuaded you to use his apartment. So many tourists go to Santa Cruz just for the *coso*. There is so much they miss. You met Manolo today, is that right? What do you think of my handsome *sobrino*?'

'He is a fine boy,' replied Tanya. 'We got on very well.'

'He is missing a mother. I keep telling Alejandro, it is time he married again.'

Alejandro looked at his sister-in-law sharply. 'And you talk too much about matters that are of no importance to Tanya.'

'Oh, but I am interested,' Tanya said. 'I agree with Beatriz that Manolo needs a mother. Have you and Inocente made any plans to get married?' She made it sound like a perfectly innocent question.

'Inocente is a friend, nothing else,' snorted Alejandro. 'I will never marry her; what put that idea into your head?'

And Beatriz looked at her in horror. 'That girl, I do

not like her, and nor does Manolo. She will not make good mother.'

Even Crisógono shook his head. 'She is not my brother's type; I do not know what he sees in her or why he ever takes her out. She is a selfish one.'

Tanya held up her hands as if trying to stop their comments. 'I'm sorry, I wasn't aware that you all had such strong feelings. I assumed——'

'You assume too much,' growled Alejandro.

'I think it is time to eat,' said Beatriz.

Despite the uproar she had caused the meal was a relaxed affair, even if Alejandro did glower at her at times, apparently still angry over her remarks about Inocente.

They started with an unusual fish soup, served carefully by a pretty girl who obviously worked for them. Tanya was impressed. Beatriz told her that the soup was made from a very old Canarian recipe. This was followed by salty pork ribs boiled together with potatoes and corn on the cob—washed down with plenty of Crisógono's *vino*.

During the course of the meal Tanya discovered that their two children were already in bed, as they, like Manolo, had missed their siesta. 'Normally, they would join us,' said Beatriz. 'It is a pity you will not see them, but—it is much quieter,' she added with a laugh.

Too full for any pudding, Tanya accepted a brandy with her coffee, which was served in a glass and was strong and black and liberally sweetened. The Canarians had a great love of sugar, she discovered— they even sugared freshly squeezed orange juice. Alejandro told her that it dated back to the islands' first export industry of sugar-cane.

Tanya was so enjoying herself that she was disappointed when Alejandro said it was time to leave— until she looked at her watch and realised it was already half-past eleven. How the time had flown! Considering she had not wanted to come out this evening, it had been extremely pleasant—probably because Beatriz and her husband were so friendly and welcoming. 'You must come again before you go back to England,' they both said as she left.

Once on their way Alejandro said sharply, 'What was all that about Inocente? you know she means nothing to me.'

'I know that's what you've told me,' she said, 'but it's not what Inocente herself feels. Surely you know that?' Or was he always blind where his women were concerned? Had he not known that she, Tanya, had once been madly in love with him? And Juanita, she too must have been in love when he left for England— yet it hadn't stopped him having an affair. And now Inocente—he was treating her with equal disregard. What type of a man was he, for goodness' sake?

'And how would you know what Inocente's feelings for me are?' he asked coldly.

Tanya lifted her shoulders. 'I've seen the way she looks at you—and the way *you* treat her,' she added scathingly. 'When you're together she means everything to you. There's more to your relationship than you're admitting.'

'If I was in love with Inocente, would I be spending my time with you?' he rasped.

Tanya eyed him coldly, although she knew he couldn't see her expression in the darkness of the car. 'I don't think you're the type of man who'll ever remain true to one woman for long.'

'Your opinion of me continues to sink, doesn't it?' he asked harshly. 'No matter how much I put myself out for you it makes no difference.'

'Why should it?' she countered. 'It's what you're like beneath the surface that counts.'

'And you think you know the true me?'

'I not only think it, I know it. You're a cheating swine, Alejandro. You cheat me, you cheat your family, you cheat Inocente, you cheated Juanita. Shall

I tell you who I feel sorry for? Manolo! Beatriz is right: he does need a mother.'

'You said earlier today that I had done a very good job in bringing him up.'

'Yes, you have, but he is still young; he should have the love of two parents. It is unfair to deprive him of a mother's love.'

'Are you suggesting yourself for the role model?' There was a sudden stillness to him, although his attention was to all outward appearances on his driving.

'Heavens, no!' Tanya cried at once. 'You're the last person I'd marry; and, according to your family, Inocente wouldn't be a very suitable candidate either. Perhaps you should look around for someone else.'

'Perhaps I don't want to look around.'

'Meaning you're happy in your single state? That you enjoy flitting from girlfriend to girlfriend, that you would be stifled if you had to settle down with one woman?' Tanya did not realise that her tone had risen, that she sounded almost shrill in the close confines of the car—not until he slammed the brakes on and brought the car to a skidding halt.

'That is enough.' He half turned in his seat towards her. 'I will not be spoken to like this.'

'The truth hurts, does it?' she taunted, her eyes locked into the glittering depths of his, feeling the full extent of his anger. But instead of being intimidated she was excited, conscious only that his sex appeal had never been stronger.

'You know nothing,' he snarled.

Tanya touched the tip of her tongue to suddenly dry lips.

'And you're certainly not the sweet, friendly girl I met in England. You're. . .' His voice tailed off, and it was almost possible to hear the hammer throb of their heartbeats. 'Hell, Tanya,' he growled thickly.

They gravitated towards each other, slowly, painfully, their eyes never leaving each other's faces, until in one final, aching, groaning moment their mouths met.

It was a deeply passionate, mutually hungry kiss, an animal hunger, a hunger born of deep-seated, unslaked desire. Tanya had never felt such an intense need, and she moved her mouth against Alejandro's, their tongues entwining, tasting, demanding.

She wanted more than this constricted place allowed; she wanted their whole bodies to meet, not just their lips. Her hands went to his head, fingers curling into the thickness of his hair, holding him, pulling, hurting, wanting, needing.

Alejandro too groaned his frustration, one hand on her chin, thumb pulling down her lower lip so that he could explore her mouth more deeply, his other hand on her back, trying to urge her closer to him.

He muttered something in Spanish beneath his breath, and then, still barely audibly, 'This is no good, Tanya, not here. We must get home, and quickly. Promise you won't go cold on me?'

'I promise.' Her eyes were like luminous blue orbs, moist, glowing, soft, reflecting her feelings, telling him without words that her need was as great as his.

Reluctantly he dragged himself away, turned the key and started the engine, put it into drive, and pulled back out on to the road. With one hand on the wheel and one hand on her thigh, her own hand covering it, he drove the rest of the way home, slowly, carefully, not wanting to break the bond that had sprung into fragile existence.

In the lift they fell upon each other again, not able to wait until they reached privacy. Lips meeting, sucking, tasting; bodies swaying, pressing, urging. Throb, throb, throb, went their hearts. Pulses raced; adrenalin ran high. Out of the lift and into the apartment, more kissing, tasting, inciting. Clothes dragged off, bodies meeting, skin inflaming.

This was what she needed, what she had ached for

since meeting him again. Tanya held nothing back —
she could not; she was out of control, drugged by this
man she had loved so many years ago. Excitement
tortured, fuelled, burned. She could hear a pounding in
her head as well as her heart, such energy, such heat.

Mouths moved to kiss and taste, to explore eyes and
ears and noses and chins. Whatever he did she did,
unthinkingly, urgently. He kissed her nipples; she
kissed his. He nipped them with his fine white teeth;
she bit his. It was an agony of hurt and pain and loving.

At what stage he carried her to the bed she did not
know, but they were lying down and he was touching
and kissing every secret inch of her, and when the
moment arrived she arched her body against his,
breathing deeply, painfully, enjoying, urging, sensing.

They both cried out at the same time, an explosion
of feeling rocking her to the very core, clinging now,
tightly, emotionally, then relaxing and lying close side
by side, holding, sighing, smiling, and finally —
sleeping.

Tanya dreamed that she was married to Alejandro,
that as well as Manolo they had children of their own,
four of them, three girls and a boy. All Canarians
loved children, she had learned, and Alejandro told
her that he wanted many. There had been no interven-
ing years; she had not married Peter. She had followed
him out to Tenerife and there had been no Juanita
waiting for him. They had been blissfully happy until
one day she had caught him with another woman in his
arms — Inocente — and her whole world collapsed.

She had gone up to the other woman and tried to
drag them apart. 'He's mine; you cannot have him.
Get away.'

'Tanya, what is wrong?' It was Alejandro's voice,
soft and puzzled.

'What are you doing with Inocente? You're mine;
she can't have you.'

'*Amor mio, amor mio*, you are dreaming.'

Tanya dragged open her heavy eyelids, and for a moment could not think where she was. Alejandro was looking at her, his expression tender and concerned. Alejandro in bed beside her! Alejandro naked! And she remembered, and colour flooded her cheeks. Last night she had drank too much of Crisógono's *vino*; last night she had let Alejandro make love to her. This morning she felt embarrassed.

'It is all right, *mi cariño*,' he murmured, stroking her hair back from her forehead. 'It was a dream, nothing more, nothing to feel worried about.'

'Oh, yes, there is. You shouldn't be here, I shouldn't have let you——'

'Shh.' He put a silencing finger to her lips. 'I am here, and it's all right, and you were right in your dream when you said I am yours. We belong together, Tanya, you and I. We should never have parted. We——'

It was Tanya's turn to interrupt. 'No, Alejandro, we do not belong. I made a mistake last night, a grave mistake.'

'How can you say that?' His fingertips brushed the soft skin of her cheek, creating a fresh surge of sensation. 'How can you say that after what we have been through together?'

'I should never have let you make love to me,' she protested. 'It was wrong; it was——'

'Hush, *bebé*, hush.' His lips covered hers, gentle this morning, his impatient hunger of the night before gone.

Instantly Tanya was lost. The old magic was back; there was nothing she could do about it. 'Oh, Alejandro,' she sighed.

'Tanya.'

They made love again, taking their time now, no hurry, just long, lazy moments of sensual pleasure, and then Tanya suddenly remembered. 'Manolo!' she exclaimed, sitting up. 'He'll wonder where you are. You must go home at once.'

'Manolo is all right,' he told her softly. 'He has a nanny, a live-in nanny; she will look after him. I told her where I was going. She would not expect me home; she knows that my brother always plies me with drink.'

Tanya relaxed again and then jumped when the telephone rang.

'I will get it,' he said. 'You lie there and look beautiful.'

He padded out of the bedroom, completely unselfconscious about his nudity, and when he returned he was smiling. 'That was Charlene. She had quite a shock when she heard my voice. She rang to say that she has managed to — er — wangle, I believe was her word, a day off, and is coming to spend it with you. What a pity. I was looking forward to a day spent together, now that we have rediscovered our feelings for each other.'

CHAPTER EIGHT

'THERE'S no need to panic,' said Alejandro, catching Tanya's arm, pulling her back as she tried to scramble out of bed. 'Your sister won't be here for another hour at least.'

'But I must be ready. I must have time to pull myself together.' She did not want Charlene seeing her with this look of love on her face. She had not seen herself in the mirror, but she knew that she was glowing; she could feel it—she could feel her eyes sparkling, her face soft and relaxed, her whole body tingling with well-being.

The love she had felt for Alejandro nine years ago had come back with a vengeance. She was a woman satisfied, a woman who knew she had satisfied her man. It was a wonderful sensation.

She allowed Alejandro to hold her for a few minutes, feeling peaceful and happy and content. Alejandro too looked relaxed and completely in tune with the world. 'Now we have rediscovered our feelings', he had said— whatever those feelings were! She still had no real idea whether he loved her or whether it was purely a physical thing on his part. She had never known, and unless he told her she never would; and it was too big a risk to take to let herself get deeply involved with him again.

She could never forget that while he had been making love to her in England Juanita had been waiting for him here. And this time it was Inocente who was waiting. The sudden note of discord in her thoughts made her wriggle uneasily.

'*Enamorada*, sweetheart, something is wrong?' His arms tightened around her, and the pressure of his body against hers was almost more than she could bear. Once more she was lost; she wanted to touch him, stroke him, make love all over again. Her heartbeats grew stronger and her throat seemed to close up, and she looked at him with her luminous blue eyes.

She could not tell him what she had been thinking, not in this moment of closeness. They were fleeting thoughts, unwanted thoughts. She loved Alejandro; that was enough, for now at least. She wanted to savour this happy feeling; she did not want to spoil it or lose it. Whatever else happened, it would be there to add to her memories of almost nine years ago.

'It's all right,' she whispered.

They lay together for another ten minutes, Alejandro leaning up on one elbow, looking at her face, stroking her nose, her eyelids, her lips, the contour of her cheeks, pushing back stray wisps of hair, murmuring soft words in his native language. Tanya hoped they were words of love; she hoped so, so very much.

At length he was the one who made the move, though he furthered the moments of intimacy by joining her in the shower, and they had only just got dressed when the doorbell rang, announcing Charlene's presence.

Tanya hugged her sister, but Charlene was looking across the room. 'I didn't expect to find you still here Alejandro.'

Tanya gasped at her insensitivity, but Alejandro merely raised an eyebrow. 'I'm sorry if I've disappointed you.'

'I hope you're going soon. It took a lot of organising to get this day off.' Charlene never believed in holding back; if she thought something, she said it.

'Don't worry, I won't spoil your day with your sister.' He spoke easily, but his mouth was suddenly grim, and Tanya knew he was thinking that Charlene had no such compunction about spoiling *his* day.

She sighed unhappily and went into the kitchen to

make coffee; Charlene followed. 'I'd have to be blind not to see what you two have been up to,' she said in a loud whisper. 'How could you, Tan, after the way he treated you?'

Tanya smiled ruefully. 'I can't help it.'

'You can't help it? He's the guy who broke your heart, for heaven's sake. Don't you remember?'

'Of course I remember, but — oh, Charlene, I know you won't understand, but the old magic's still there. I only have to look at him and I go weak at the knees.'

Charlene shook her head. 'You're going to get hurt again. He has another girlfriend, in case you'd forgotten.'

'He says she means nothing to him.'

'Nothing, my eye. You surely don't believe him?'

'I don't know. All I know is that I love him and there's nothing I can do about it.'

'Of course there is,' cried Charlene. 'You can get out of here for a start. You ought to have known he wouldn't leave you alone. The guy's a womaniser of the highest order. I wouldn't trust him as far as I could throw him.'

'You say the sweetest things, Charlene.' Alejandro had come into the kitchen behind them. 'Don't you think you should leave Tanya to make up her own mind?'

'Not where you're concerned,' snapped the older girl. 'You did the dirty on her once; I don't want it happening again.'

'*I* did the dirty?' A frown scoured his brow. 'As I recall, Tanya was the one who walked out on me.'

'And you — '

'Oh, shut up, you two,' interrupted Tanya. 'You're spoiling my holiday.'

Her sister grimaced. 'I'm sorry; it's just that I'm disappointed in you.'

'I think, Charlene,' said Alejandro, walking over to

Tanya and putting his arm about her shoulders, 'that your sister is capable of making up her own mind.'

It was going to be a difficult day, thought Tanya wearily. She wished Charlene hadn't come. She wished she could have spent it alone with Alejandro. Before her sister arrived she had been on top of the world; now she was slowly sliding down, and she did not want to. She wanted to stay up there; she wanted to retain these feelings, savour them, remember them.

She made the coffee strong, the way Alejandro liked it, and got out rolls and butter.

'Can you imagine Peter eating something like this for breakfast?' asked Charlene with a wicked laugh. 'He was an egg and bacon man, Alejandro, very much a traditionalist.'

'Is that so?' he asked, and there was a sudden edge to his tone.

Tanya wished her sister had not brought Peter's name into the conversation.

But Charlene was not finished yet. 'Oh, yes, he was a stickler for all things proper, wasn't he, Tan?'

Tanya smiled weakly and nodded.

'For instance he would never have stayed the night with Tanya before they were married. He loved her too much; he wouldn't have thought it proper.'

Alejandro pushed back his chair and stood up, dark eyes savage. 'I think I should go.'

'What's wrong?' taunted Charlene. 'Can't you bear to hear me talk about Peter? He was a fine man without a doubt, and Tanya was devastated when he died. They were so much in love.'

'Charlene, shut up,' hissed Tanya through grated teeth.

'Why, when it's the truth? Don't you ever talk about Peter to Alejandro? Don't you ever tell him what a good marriage you had? You'll never find another man as good as he was.'

Tanya knew why Charlene was saying these things,

but that did not stop her being appalled, and when Alejandro spun round on his heel and left the room, his face tense, she followed him out to the lift. 'I apologise for Charlene's outspokenness,' she said. 'She had no right saying those things.'

'But I've no doubt they were true.' Gone was the gentleness, the caring, replaced by a stone-cold anger. 'I hadn't realised how much you loved your husband. I think I should perhaps be grateful to Charlene for opening my eyes.'

'It's perfectly natural I should love the man I married,' she told him, feeling a rising anger too. Why should it make any difference? People could love again, couldn't they?

'It sounds as though your feelings for Peter went far deeper than they ever did for me.' His eyes blazed coldly into hers, testing, questioning, awaiting her response.

Tanya turned away, disappointed and confused. In a matter of seconds the magic spell had been broken.

His hand on her shoulder spun her round. 'I'm waiting, Tanya.' And his clipped tones were like a knife in her heart. 'Don't be afraid to tell me the truth.'

'There is more than one kind of love,' she said huskily. 'What I felt for Peter——'

'Was so strong that you cannot forget it,' he snarled. 'Is that what you were going to say? Could I be right in thinking that last night and this morning your thoughts were with Peter and not me, that it was his body you were drowning in, not mine, that you only gave yourself to me because you still ache with love for this man I did not know? I think I have a lot to thank Charlene for. It would appear I was in danger of making a fool of myself for the second time.'

The lift came, and without another word he stepped into it. Tanya walked slowly back to the apartment, feeling rejected and disappointed and hurt, and extremely angry with her sister.

'I guess that put him in his place,' said Charlene with satisfaction.

Tanya glared, her blue eyes fierce. 'You had no right talking about Peter like that.'

'It needed something to get that star-struck look out of your eyes. Really, Tan, you need your head examining for falling for Alejandro all over again. I know he's got charm, oodles of it, but the truth is he's a two-timing creep. I've actually done you a favour. He didn't like it, did he? He didn't like hearing about Peter.'

'Nor did I,' snapped Tanya.

'Surely you're not trying to forget him?' Charlene frowned. 'You're not trying to replace him with Alejandro?'

'I'll never forget Peter,' she replied. 'He'll always have a special place in my heart. But there's nothing to stop me falling in love again.'

'With that swine?'

'You don't know him, Charlene.'

'I know what he did to you, and I'll never forgive him — and nor should you. He's not serious, you know. He's duping you again; he's playing with you. Can't you see what he's like?'

Tanya closed her eyes. This was a side to Alejandro that she had blacked out of her mind for the last twelve hours. She did not want to think about it. He had seemed to be genuinely fond of her; it had gone further than simple attraction, hadn't it? It was why he was so hurt; he felt let down by Charlene's deliberate comments. And there hadn't been time to talk to him, to tell him that he meant more to her than Peter ever had. *More to her*! The thought stood out in her mind in neon lights. It was true. She was deeply and irrevocably in love. It had never gone away.

'Tanya?'

'I see him differently from you, Charlene. I know I was hurt and upset all those years ago, and I said I hated him, but—well, I don't any more, and nothing you can say will make any difference.'

'The real question, then, is, does he love you?' Charlene looked at her sister with concern in her eyes. 'And I think we both know the answer to that. He isn't capable of loving. When I said he was a womaniser I meant it. He might let you think he loves you, but I expect he does that to all the girls he takes out. Be careful, Tanya, please. I don't want you hurt again.'

There was no more said after that. They went to the same beach as yesterday, they had lunch at the apartment, they strolled around Santa Cruz, idly watching the election of the old-age pensioner *carnaval* queen. They went back to the apartment and changed, and Charlene took her to a popular restaurant in Esperanza.

It had been a long day, thought Tanya, when she finally went to bed. Charlene had tried to persuade her to return to Matilde's, but she had been adamant. 'I came up here to see the *carnaval*, every little bit of it, I'm not going to miss out now.'

And so, with an admonition to be careful, Charlene had left, driving away in her smart white car.

The bed felt empty without Alejandro, the night never-ending. Tanya kept hoping he might ring, but the phone remained silent, and she woke the next morning feeling thoroughly dejected. Even the weather reflected her mood, the jagged peaks of the mountains hidden behind a grey curtain of rain.

She stayed in all day, alone, miserable, willing Alejandro to contact her, wanting to make amends, to explain her feelings, to repair the rift Charlene had torn in their delicate relationship.

He had left her a programme of events for the *carnaval*, and tonight was the *carnaval* queen gala heats—and if Alejandro was a member of the jury, as he put it, then she wouldn't be seeing him tonight either!

She toyed with the idea of going anyway, but as there was no sign of the rain letting up there was really no sense in getting wet when she probably wouldn't even see Alejandro. She decided to watch it on television instead.

It was late afternoon when the skies cleared, when the fangs of the Anaga Mountains stood out in sharp relief against a haze of blue. She would go for a walk; she had had enough of sitting indoors, beautiful though the apartment was.

Before she had even fetched her jacket from the wardrobe a knock came on the door, a loud, peremptory knock, and she knew it was Alejandro, still sounding as though he was in a bad mood. But at least he was here; she could talk to him, explain, make him understand that Charlene had been deliberately trying to cause mischief.

Her heartbeats drummed painfully and she pinned a smile of welcome to her lips as she opened the door, and even though Alejandro's face looked like thunder she still kept smiling as she stood back for him to enter. 'I'm so glad you've come.' He had on a crisp white shirt and dark trousers, as though he'd been out on business all day. He looked devastatingly handsome, and triggered everything inside her into vibrant life.

'The only reason I'm here,' he said, the moment the door closed, 'is because I feel responsible for you.' He walked across to the wide window with its panoramic views over the capital.

'You don't have to feel guilty,' Tanya flared in sudden anger. She had been hoping for an apology, at least a suggestion they talk. 'I don't mind being alone.'

He turned round slowly and faced her, his brown eyes cool, a faint frown between his brows. 'Have you been out today?'

'No,' she admitted, 'but only because of the weather. As a matter of fact I was just about to go for a walk.'

'Then I'll join you. I think we should talk.' Still no hint that he was pleased to see her.

'What about?' asked Tanya.

'Us. You and me. You and Peter. Your feelings.'

'How about yours?' she countered sharply.

'Mine too, if you like,' he replied with an indifferent lift of his shoulders.

Tanya felt a faint surge of hope. He was prepared to discuss *his* feelings. Maybe now they would get somewhere.

They left the apartment in silence, descended to the ground floor in silence, Alejandro standing straight and tall and unapproachable, Tanya's heartbeats hurried, every one of her senses alert and responsive. How could he ignore her like this after the passion of their lovemaking? How could he turn his feelings on and off because of a few ill-chosen words?

The lift doors opened and they walked out into the sunshine, but Alejandro's reserve did not melt. They strolled side by side, mingling with happy, voluble Santacruceros, all in party mood. They were probably the only two who weren't smiling. *Carnaval* fever had taken over everyone during this pre-Lenten festival. Banks and shops were closed; the whole city was out celebrating.

Tanya thought they were heading towards the port, but instead he led the way into a park, which was a welcome oasis of greenery among all the offices and apartment blocks. Tropical trees and flowers grew in abundance: bottlebrush, with its racemes of scarlet flowers, jacaranda vivid with clusters of purple, yellow mimosa, even a red poinsettia as tall as herself, which she found totally amazing, because she had only ever seen it as a houseplant.

'Why, Tanya, why?' he asked as they walked slowly along the path.

'Why what?' She turned to look at him, saw the

disapproving frown between his brows, the grimness to his lips, and she ached for the rapport of two days ago.

'Why did you let me make love to you?'

It was a loaded question, and Tanya knew a lot depended on her answer. 'Because—I couldn't help myself,' she said slowly, hesitantly. 'Because I wanted to.'

'Were you thinking of Peter?' He looked straight ahead as he spoke, and she saw a muscle jerking in his jaw, a sure sign of inner tension.

'Did I behave as though I was thinking of another man?' She wanted him to believe that she had been genuine in her response without her having to put it into words.

'I suppose not, but who really understands the vagaries of a woman's mind?'

'I am what you see,' she told him. 'I don't know what type of woman you normally associate with, but I can assure you that I don't hide behind anything.'

They paused to look at a statue of a solidly built woman with large, pendulous breasts and a scrap of material covering her loins. She was half hidden in the mist from a fountain and was somewhat the worse for wear, but nevertheless her nudity managed to arouse in Tanya some of the feelings she had felt the night before last.

There had been no coyness, no embarrassment at stripping off in front of him—it had all seemed so natural, so right, and yet now he was accusing her of having false emotions.

'I wouldn't like to think that you did, Tanya, but after what your sister said——'

She stopped him with a sharp outburst. 'Charlene was out to cause trouble, that's all. If you prefer to believe her, then this conversation is pointless.' She swung round on her heel and began to walk back the way they had come. She was disappointed in him, outraged in fact that he still thought the worst of her.

She had never questioned *him*, even though thoughts of Juanita were often uppermost in her mind.

He caught up with her. 'There are so many unanswered questions, Tanya.'

'And do any of them really matter?' she riposted, her eyes the same vivid blue as the sky. 'Why can't we accept that things have happened in our lives that neither of us were happy about at the time? Why can't we accept that the past is just that, over and done with? Why can't we forget everything and — and begin all over again?' She was baring her soul here, letting him know that she was still attracted to him.

'You mean that?'

Tanya nodded.

'You're willing to forget that I've been married?'

'Yes.'

'You're willing to forget Inocente?'

Tanya paused. 'That depends on whether you see her again.'

'I'll naturally have to see her to tell her it's all over between us.'

'So there was something?' she accused, eyes narrowing.

'Inocente thought so.'

'But you didn't; you were playing her along?' The same as he had her all those years ago? Was she making a terrible mistake in suggesting they start to see each other again? Could Charlene be right — he was not to be trusted?

Alejandro's breath came out on a surge of impatience. 'I am not "playing her along", as you put it. Inocente knows what my feelings for her are; she's simply hoping that they'll change.'

'And meantime she's pleasant company? Have you ever taken her to bed?' The moment the question was out Tanya wished she could retract it. She was the one who had said let bygones be bygones, and yet here she was asking questions that she had no right asking. But she wanted to know. This was too immediate. It wasn't like Peter or Juanita; this was now, a girl in his present life. She had a right to know what was going on between them.

'As a matter of fact, no,' he answered, 'though I don't expect you'll believe me. You seem to have it firmly fixed in your mind that we're having a raging affair.'

'Inocente has always given that impression, but nevertheless, if you tell me it's not so, then I believe you.'

They had left the park now and were strolling between high-rise apartments. It was not such a relaxing atmosphere, and Tanya regretted turning back. She would have liked to seal their new agreement with a kiss but there was no chance of that here, there were far too many people milling around.

'Let's go back to the apartment,' he said gruffly, and Tanya remembered the last time he had said that—and where it had led! It was as though someone had suddenly put a match to her, lighting her up from inside, and there was a lift to her step as hand in hand they retraced their steps. Suddenly the future looked rosy.

As they stood waiting for the lift he took her face between his palms and gently kissed her. The doors opened and they turned together—and Inocente stood watching them! The woman's eyes were filled with pure hatred as they turned upon Tanya. She was wearing a tight, cream, linen suit which showed off her sensual body, and extremely high-heeled shoes which made her legs look very long.

Alejandro was the first to speak. 'Inocente, what are you doing here?' He spoke in English, forcing her to do the same.

'What does it look like?' Her eyes softened as she looked at him. 'I came to see you, *amor mio*. I knew you were one of the jury this evening. I guessed I would find you here, but I did not expect to find you — otherwise engaged. What is — Tanya doing here?' She somehow managed to make her name sound like a dirty word.

'Tanya is my guest for the duration of the *carnaval*,' he answered patiently.

'She is staying in your apartment?' Inocente's wide eyes opened even further.

'That is right. Would you care to come up and join us for afternoon tea? It's a little late, I'm afraid, because ——'

'No, I would not,' snapped the dark-haired girl viciously, 'but I would like to talk to you.'

'For a few minutes,' he agreed, and, turning to Tanya, said softly, 'Would you mind very much going up alone? I won't be long, I promise.' He touched her chin in a gentle, affectionate gesture.

What if she said no? What would he say then? Tanya was furious. Just as they had started to get back on a sound footing this woman had turned up and spoiled everything. But she kept her feelings well-hidden, smiling at him warmly, touching his face too. 'I'll look forward to it,' she said huskily.

She entered the lift without a glance at Inocente, trying to look every inch a woman in love, a woman confident of her man. In actual truth she wasn't, not at all. This woman was clever and probably knew Alejandro far better than she did. She would know how to wind him round her little finger. He had said he would tell her it was all over, but Tanya doubted whether Inocente would accept it. This was probably the end. He would come up and tell her that he could not keep his word — Inocente might even come with him to make sure that she got her marching orders.

Dejectedly she sat down on the beautiful soft leather settee, thinking that she would never see a white settee again without remembering this moment. What hurt most was that Inocente had come to his apartment to

find him, and yet Alejandro had told her that he had
invited no one here. So how had she known about it?
It was clear she could believe nothing he said.

It was an age before he returned. Tanya was even
toying with the idea of packing her suitcase and
demanding that he take her back to Matilde's. None of
it was worth the heartache. Then he walked in the
door. 'Tanya, *mi cariño*, I am so sorry to have kept
you waiting. Inocente was not so easy to handle as I
imagined.'

'You mean she wouldn't accept the fact that you
want to finish with her?' Tanya rose and faced him, no
warmth or pleasure in her face. 'I didn't really think
she would; she's the clinging vine type. But you don't
have to worry. I've had time to sit and think. It
wouldn't have worked; we're completely incompatible,
you and I.'

'Incompatible?' He looked baffled by this sudden
attack.

'Except where things physical are concerned, of
course, but where would that get us? Nowhere at all.
Once you'd got it out of your system I'd be dumped
again. No, Alejandro, I think it would be better all
round if I went back to Matilde's for the rest of my
holiday.'

'You're not serious?' His frown was deep, his eyes
darkly incredulous. 'Tanya—you have it all wrong.
Inocente has gone. It is over, finished; she finally
accepted it.'

Tanya swallowed hard. She wanted to believe him
but was not sure if she could. It was all so delicate, this
relationship of theirs. She felt as though she were
poised on a knife-edge all the time.

'You do not believe me?' He looked troubled by her
attitude.

'I'd like to, but from what little I've seen of Inocente
I didn't think she'd give you up that easily.'

'It wasn't easy, I agree,' he said 'but it's done now;

you can forget her.' He took her into his arms and held her for several long moments, stroking the honey-gold of her hair, soothing, relaxing, instilling peace into her, until finally Tanya lifted her head and smiled into his face.

'That's better,' he murmured, and he lifted her chin, pressing a kiss to her mouth. 'My beautiful Tanya, don't ever doubt anything I tell you. I would never lie.'

Except by omission, she thought. He had never told her about Juanita, and she would not have found out if she hadn't seen the letter from his father. But she believed now that he had told Inocente the truth, and she was happy in his arms, accepting his kiss, responding, holding him too, letting him see by actions rather than words that she believed him.

The gala heats began at nine-thirty, and Alejandro told her that Beatriz and Crisógono were coming so she would not be alone. They had a light meal of an omelette beforehand and, even though they thought they had plenty of time, when they got to the square it was almost time for the event to start.

Alejandro spotted his brother on the second row and left Tanya to make her way to them. 'I'll see you later when it's all over,' he murmured, his mouth close to hers, one last, intimate kiss exchanged.

Tanya felt on top of the world again, watching him walk away. Lord, he was magnificent: tall, imposing, exciting, standing out from the crowd. And he was hers! There had been no words of love exchanged as yet, and he hadn't made love to her again, but she was confident now. It was all coming together. She loved him and——

A hand tapping her shoulder made her spin around, and there was Inocente, black eyes blazing, two spots of high colour in her cheeks. 'You are looking very sure of yourself, but I can guarantee that whatever Alejandro told you it is not true.'

'Really?' Tanya lifted her chin, trying her hardest to

look disdainful, even though her heart was stammering uneasily. 'And why would he lie?'

'To keep you happy — until you go back to England. And then ——' she paused to add emphasis to her words, ' — he will be mine again.'

CHAPTER NINE

INOCENTE sounded so confident that Tanya felt like believing her, but Alejandro had been adamant that it was all over. The girl was lying; she had to be. 'I think you're wrong,' she said coldly. 'Alejandro and I have reached an understanding. You're no longer a part of his life, and he told you that. Why won't you accept it?'

'Because I know what he feels for you will not last. He has had other girls before, but always he has come back to me, and he always will. So you see, you are wasting your time.'

This sounded dangerously close to the truth—it was exactly what had happened to her in England—but surely Alejandro wouldn't do the dirty on her a second time? Surely she could believe that his feelings for her were genuine, that this time it was going to be a permanent relationship?

'You're lying,' she said sharply. 'It's yourself you're trying to convince, not me.' There were crowds all around them, but she was conscious of nothing except this woman with bright red lips and fingernails like talons.

Inocente gave a shrug of her narrow shoulders. 'If you do not believe me, wait and see. It will happen, I can promise you. Alejandro and I go back a long way; we are close, *very* close. I have spent many happy hours here in his apartment, as well as at his home in Orotava. There is nothing I do not know about him, and it is a fact that one day soon you will be—how do you say it in England?—you will be history.'

There was contempt in the woman's tone, a curl to her lips, and Tanya felt cold inside. She was strongly

inclined to believe Inocente — it went along with everything she knew about Alejandro, but still she kept her
chin high. 'You can say what you like; I shall not
believe you. Alejandro and I——'

'Tanya! *Tanya!*' Beatriz's voice, loud and clear,
reached her from her seat several yards away. 'Come
along; you will miss the beginning.'

Relief shuddered through her as she caught Beatriz's
eye. 'Excuse me,' she said to Inocente. 'I must go.'

'Don't think you are going to win,' spat the other
girl, 'just because you have got his family on your side.
Alejandro loves me, and it will not be long now before
he asks me to marry him.' With a toss of her head, her
thick black hair swinging across her face, she turned
and marched away.

Tanya felt herself trembling, though whether it was
with anger or relief that the confrontation was over,
she did not know. Damn Inocente and her vicious
tongue. Again she was left feeling extremely unsure of
herself.

She squeezed past a row of people to the vacant seat
Beatriz had kept for her, sinking into it with relief,
unaware that her face had gone deathly pale.

'What was Inocente saying to you?' Beatriz's face
was full of concern.

Tanya grimaced. 'She was warning me off your
brother-in-law. Thank you for rescuing me.'

A torrent of angry Spanish flowed from the woman's
lips, finishing finally, 'That girl, she is bad. You must
not listen. Alejandro is a fool for getting involved with
her. I tell him so, many times, but he take no notice.
What it is about her I do not know, but she is evil. She
has her — what do you say? — she has her nails stuck in
him and she will not let go.'

Crisógono nodded his agreement. 'Beatriz is right;
Inocente is no good. I wonder what she's doing here.'

'She came to see Alejandro,' Tanya told him. 'We
met her earlier outside his apartment.'

'And she didn't take kindly to seeing you with him?' Crisógono nodded his understanding. 'That explains her attack. Don't let it worry you, Tanya. It's very clear to both Beatriz and me whom he prefers. We said so the other night after you'd gone, didn't we?' he asked his wife. 'I haven't seen my brother so happy in a long time.'

And then the proceedings started and there was no time for further conversation.

Tanya was enthralled by it all, and absolutely astounded by the lavishness and size of the costumes. Beatriz told her that they took many, many months to complete. 'They are made by top dress designers who guard their creations with their life. The dresses have to be hinged so that they can get through the stage doors, because the designers will not even tell the organisers their dimensions. Sometimes it is difficult even for the girl to walk.'

Tanya could see this for herself as each girl paraded about the stage. On occasions, as the contestant turned to walk this way and that, male assistants had to lift the dress and turn it for her. The girl herself was almost hidden inside a startling creation of feathers and sequins and silks of all hues and shapes.

Even with the girl's arms outstretched, the skirt of the costume was still at least another metre each side of her, and her striking head-dress was so tall and unwieldy that it was a wonder it stayed in place, or that her neck was strong enough to stand the weight. Each design was different, resembling a fine bird of paradise, a peacock, a butterfly, a dragon, a tree, or nothing at all, just a glittering display that took your breath away.

'To make, they cost millions of pesetas,' Beatriz informed her. 'Different Canarian companies sponsor them, and the girls, they spend many hours in the *gimnasio* preparing themselves for the weight of the dresses.'

Tanya could well believe this. She had never seen

anything so extravagant as these 'dresses' in all her life; they made the dresses sewn by Matilde look very simple indeed.

The girls were beautiful also. Tanya had a sudden image of Alejandro watching them, eyeing them up and down. How could he not be attracted? From the waist up the girls were virtually naked, except for a spangly creation barely covering their breasts. They swayed gently to the music — as far as the weight of their outfits would let them — smiling all the time, their eyes sparkling, inviting.

Jealousy seared through her. Would he be tempted by any of them? Would any of them be his next victim? *Victim*! Was that how she saw herself? The word had crept into her mind unawares, but it showed how little she trusted him, how Inocente had poisoned her mind. But so too had Charlene. Both, in their own way, had warned her off Alejandro. Shouldn't she take some notice at least?

'Something is wrong?'

Tanya discovered that Beatriz was watching her face, seeing the conflicting emotions.

'You are not enjoying it?'

'Yes, yes, of course I am,' Tanya answered immediately. 'It was just a thought — nothing to do with the gala.'

'It is Inocente who has upset you, yes?'

Tanya lifted her shoulders, 'A little.'

Beatriz shook her head angrily. 'More than a little, I would say; you must try to forget her. Do you love Alejandro?'

Beatriz's direct question shocked Tanya, and she looked at the other woman, wide-eyed. 'Is it obvious?'

'To me, yes,' said the woman, smiling softly. 'Because I love him too, as a brother-in-law, of course. He is a fine man, if a little stupid sometimes where the female sex is concerned — and I do not mean you, Tanya. You are different; you would be good for him.

You are not interested in him for his money, like a lot of other girls, like Inocente. That is all she is after, I am sure.'

'I've never thought much about money,' Tanya agreed. She hadn't even known that Alejandro was wealthy. Oh, he had the trappings now all right, but there had been no expensive car or designer clothes all those years ago. What did money matter where love was concerned? It certainly didn't matter to her.

'Are you seeing Alejandro later, when the judging is over?' asked Beatriz.

'He said so,' Tanya acknowledged. Unless Inocente waylaid him first! She could see the other girl standing several yards away, apparently intent on the beautiful girls and their floating dresses, but frequently glancing in Tanya's direction. Occasionally their eyes met, and there was such venom on the dark girl's face that Tanya felt as though she were being beaten to the ground.

'Then we will have to make sure that you get to him before Inocente.' Beatriz glanced fiercely across at where the other girl was standing.

Tanya had not realised that Beatriz had spotted Inocente, but now the girl looked across and saw both pairs of eyes in her direction. Her chin came up, her black hair was tossed, and a supremely confident smile curved her lips. I know what you're thinking, she seemed to say, but I shall get to him first, don't worry.

Beatriz swore beneath her breath and her hand caught hold of Tanya's, squeezing tightly. The heats drew to an end, there was a surge of movement from the audience, and Tanya lost sight of Inocente. Beatriz swept her along and whether it was by good luck or genuine management, Alejandro was suddenly at their side.

'Did you enjoy that, *mi cariño*?' he asked with a gentle smile, his hand finding hers and holding it firmly.

'Yes, it was most enjoyable. They were wonderful creations.'

'Weren't they indeed? How the girls manage to walk in them I don't know.'

'They were very pretty girls. Have you made up your mind who's to be in the finals?'

'You didn't hear it announced?' He frowned faintly.

Tanya shook her head. 'I'm afraid Beatriz and I were talking.'

'I should have known.' His face lightened. 'Beatriz likes to talk, and always at the wrong time. Never mind, you will see the finalists tomorrow. I have already made up my mind who I would like to win, but, of course, I am not the only member of the jury.'

Tanya tried to imagine which girl it was he had decided would make a suitable queen of the *carnaval*, and in so doing felt another stab of jealousy. It was silly, she knew, but she could not help it. She simply did not trust him. And how could a relationship succeed without trust?

As they followed the crowds Tanya caught a glimpse of an evil-looking Inocente. Her eyes were on Alejandro and she did not even notice Tanya watching her, and Alejandro, Tanya was pleased to note, did not even see the girl. Beatriz did, though, and carefully steered their small party in a different direction, and very soon Inocente was out of sight.

'Are you coming back to the apartment, Cris?' Alejandro asked his brother.

But both he and his wife shook their head. 'We must get home; besides, I'm sure you'd much prefer to be alone with Tanya.'

Tanya was suddenly not sure that she wanted to be alone with Alejandro. It was this thing called trust that was bothering her. Inocente had sounded so very sure that they would get back together once she, Tanya, had returned to England. And he had said nothing about seeing her again once her holiday was over, nothing about a continued relationship. It really did seem as though he was interested only in the here and now.

They strolled hand in hand through the streets, and everywhere people were laughing and talking excitedly. 'You're very quiet,' remarked Alejandro as they ascended in the high-speed lift to his apartment.

'I'm tired,' she lied.

'Then I won't keep you up any longer. You have enjoyed tonight?'

'Yes.'

'Beatriz and Cris looked after you?'

'Of course.'

'I thought you looked a bit strained.'

Tanya shrugged. 'There's nothing wrong that a good night's sleep won't put right.' Except that she doubted she would sleep. Her mind was too active, too distressed.

At the apartment door he hesitated. 'I want to come in, but I know that if I do it will be impossible to leave, and I promised Manolo I would be there in the morning to tell him all about tonight.'

He took her face between his palms and kissed first her forehead, then the tip of her nose, and finally her lips.

Tanya felt the usual flood of sensations, but she could not respond. Inocente's confident words, and her vindictive expression, were too vivid in her mind.

Alejandro held her from him and frowned. 'There *is* something wrong. Tanya, you must tell me; I want no more barriers between us.'

She wanted to tell him what Inocente had said, she wanted to hear him deny it, but what if he didn't? Perhaps tomorrow she would feel better. She would have sorted out the conflict in her mind, she might even feel able to give him the benefit of the doubt, but not now, not tonight, not while Inocente's malevolent face loomed large in her mind's eye.

'Alejandro, I promise you, it's just tiredness. It's not been an easy day.'

'My fault because I was angry with you,' he said sorrowfully. He slid his hand beneath the fall of her hair to her nape, his thumb caressing the soft skin behind her ear. 'I neglected you; left you here all alone. I apologise. The truth is I was jealous of your husband, and the love you felt for him. I could not think of you without picturing you together, you in his arms making love.'

And now *she* was jealous of Inocente and all those other girls he had been watching so closely tonight. Not Juanita; Juanita was his past. But he was, after all, a healthy, full-blooded male, more sensual than most. How could he fail to be attracted by them? By any girl? She already knew that he could not remain faithful to one girl at a time; always he had two on the go. How could she have faith in him?

He bent and kissed her again, his lips brushing hers gently. '*Buenas noches, mi corazón*. Tomorrow we will spend the whole day together, I promise you. Go now and get your beauty sleep.'

Tanya nodded, smiling weakly. 'Goodnight, Alejandro.'

As she had known, sleep did not come easily, and when she did manage to drop off she had nightmarish dreams about Inocente. She woke soon after seven, feeling that she had not slept at all.

She had just made herself a strong cup of coffee when the telephone rang. 'Tanya, I have bad news.' Alejandro's deep voice sounded in her ear. 'There is some sort of trouble at the packing plant; I must go and sort it out.'

In one way she felt relieved, in another desperate because she had another day to get through alone. She pulled a wry face to herself. 'It's all right, Alejandro; you do whatever you have to do.'

'Did you not sleep well, Tanya? You still sound weary.'

'I suppose I am,' she agreed. 'I was over-tired actually. I hardly slept at all.'

'Have I woken you, *mi cariño*?'

'No, no, I was making myself a drink.'

'Then I suggest you take it to bed with you and try to get a few more hours. You'll have another late night tonight at the finals.'

Tanya was not sure whether she wanted to go again. Was the pleasure of seeing the scintillating costumes worth the torment of visualising Alejandro with these girls? 'Will Beatriz be there again?' she asked.

'But of course. It is an annual event for them, notwithstanding the fact that one of the finalists is Beatriz's cousin.'

'Really? She never said.' On the other hand, they had been talking about Inocente so much that they had discussed little else. Was this the one he favoured? Was she as beautiful as Beatriz? Actually, all the girls were beautiful, and she could not blame him for showing an interest in these lovely Canarian girls, Inocente included. With her own fair complexion and golden hair she felt quite pale and uninteresting beside them.

And why was she getting paranoid? He had chosen her; he had been attracted to her in England; he had, he said, given up Inocente. Why was she worrying? 'I'll be ready when you come,' she said, but her voice was strained.

When the doorbell sounded later in the morning she sprang up to open it. When she saw Inocente she could not believe her eyes. Not this woman again.

'If you've come looking for Alejandro he's not here,' she said sharply.

'Yes, I know, I've just left him,' announced Inocente with satisfaction.

Tanya felt a fierce pain stab her heart. So Alejandro had been lying when he said it was business keeping him away. It was Inocente, this girl he insisted he had finished with! This was the type of business he meant.

'He asked me to tell you that he won't be able to make it today after all. He said you might as well go out and enjoy the sunshine instead of sitting around.'

A chill stole down Tanya's spine. He had asked Inocente to pass on this message instead of ringing her again himself! 'Will he be here for the gala queen final tonight?' Her voice was little more than a whisper.

Inocente lifted her slender shoulders. 'I expect so; he takes his duties as a member of the jury seriously, but I imagine he will be leaving straight away again afterwards.'

Meaning he would not have time for her! How much of this was true and how much Inocente had made up Tanya was not sure. Only of one thing was she sure: he would not be coming here today.

'Thank you for telling me,' she said, her chin high, trying not to show her distress.

'It is my pleasure.' With a satisfied smile the girl turned and headed back towards the lift.

Tanya closed the door quietly, fighting the urge to slam it. Damn Inocente! Damn Alejandro! Between them they were playing some kind of game with her. Well she *would* go out; she would go out all day and she wouldn't go to the finals. If he looked for her he wouldn't find her, and, if he didn't like it, too bad. He should have apologised himself instead of letting Inocente pass on his message.

If it hadn't been for the fact that she wanted to see the grand parade on Shrove Tuesday, and the firework display afterwards, she would have taken a bus back to Matilde's right there and then, and if he thought he was going to come to her tomorrow and console her with apologies he could think again.

The telephone rang but she did not answer; it could only be Charlene, and she did not want to speak to her. She picked up her bag and left the apartment, this time getting a great deal of satisfaction out of slamming the door.

It was a long day and an even longer evening. In the end she did go to the gala queen finals, but she stood well out of sight and melted into the crowd the instant the decision was announced.

She did not want to go back to the apartment yet in case Alejandro came looking for her, but where was there to go at this time of night? Until suddenly she heard her name called. 'Tanya, it is you, isn't it?' She looked across and saw Juan smiling at her. 'What are you doing here alone?' he asked. 'Where is Alejandro?'

'I've no idea,' she answered with a shrug of her shoulders

Juan frowned. 'But I thought you and my cousin were very close. I thought ——'

'You thought wrong,' she interrupted sharply.

'Charlene told me that you had resumed your relationship of however many years ago it was.'

'Charlene must have got the wrong impression.'

'But you are staying in Alejandro's apartment?'

'It doesn't mean a thing. It was a generous gesture on his part, that's all.'

'In that case you won't have any objections to joining me for a drink?'

'Not at all.' Tanya smiled easily. This was the answer to her prayers.

Juan spent the next hour talking about Charlene, extolling her virtues, leaving Tanya in no doubt that he had fallen for her sister very badly, and when he finally took her back to the apartment she felt that she was safe from Alejandro.

At the door Juan bade her goodnight, and she did not put the light on until she had closed it behind her. She had the shock of her life when she saw Alejandro standing in the middle of the floor waiting for her, his face thunderous, his whole body rigid with anger.

'Where the devil have you been?' The furious words

were thrust across the room. 'Do you not care that I have been out of my mind with worry?' I rang Matilde, I rang your sister, I was thinking of telephoning the police.'

'What do you mean, where have I been?' demanded Tanya crossly. 'A more pertinent question would be, what are you doing here? I understood I wouldn't be seeing you today.'

'I said I was busy this morning.' A black scowl darkened his features. 'I telephoned; I came. You were missing, gone; no message, nothing.' His eyes were piercingly sharp. 'I even thought you might have left altogether until I checked your clothes. Where the hell have you been, and whose voice was that I heard? Someone you picked up? *Maldito sea*, Tanya, how can you do this to me?'

She lifted her chin in her usual defensive manner. 'It wasn't a stranger, as a matter of fact; it was your cousin.'

'Manuel again? I thought you said there was nothing going on there.'

'Not Manuel, Juan.'

'Juan?' he asked with a frown.

'That's right,' she agreed coolly. 'It isn't a crime, is it, to have a drink with someone else?' Lord, why was he so angry when all this was his doing?

'Have you been with him all day?' The questions were fired at her like bullets from a gun.

'Goodness, no. I only met him an hour ago in the square.'

'You were there? But Cris said they hadn't seen you.'

'I didn't sit with them.'

'But why?'

'You should know the answer to that,' she returned bitterly.

His frown deepened. 'You'd better explain.'

'What is there to say, expect that I would have

thought more of you if you'd given me your excuses in person?'

'You're not making sense, Tanya.'

She sighed impatiently and moved further into the room. 'I'm talking about Inocente. Why send a message with her? Why didn't you tell me yourself that you couldn't make it?'

'You've seen Inocente?' His eyes narrowed questioningly.

'It would appear that so did you,' she riposted. 'And to think that I believed your excuse.'

'Tanya.' He took her by the shoulders and looked deep into her eyes. 'I have not seen Inocente today.'

She ripped herself free before his nearness could destroy her. 'Don't lie to me, Alejandro.'

'It is the truth,' he insisted. 'Tanya, look at me.' He caught hold of her again. 'Why would I lie about something like that?'

'You tell me,' she spat, avoiding his eyes. They would be her undoing.

'I wouldn't lie to you.'

'No?' Her brows rose sceptically. 'I'm afraid I don't believe you.'

'But you believed Inocente?'

'Why would she tell lies?' Tanya asked. 'Why would she say *you* had sent her? She must have known I would find out whether she was speaking the truth.'

'She would lie to split us up, Tanya.'

Tanya eyed him coldly. 'If you haven't seen her today, then explain how she knew that you'd already phoned me. It made perfect sense when she said that you wouldn't be able to make it after all.'

He shook his head. 'I do not know how she knew, but rest assured I will find out.' Then his tone softened. '*Mi cariño*, how could you think this of me?'

Quite easily, thought Tanya. It was difficult to trust him completely when he had let her down so badly in the past. 'Inocente sounded very sincere.'

'Inocente was extremely angry when I finished with her. I did not realise it at the time, but it is obvious she will go to any lengths to put an end to our relationship. She sees you as the person who has come between me and her. The truth of the matter is that I never had any serious intentions where Inocente was concerned.'

The same as he had never had any serious intentions about her all those years ago. The question was, had he now? Or was she as much a game to him as Inocente had been? Was this how he treated all his women? When someone else took his fancy was the last one dumped? Maybe she ought to ask him.

But before she could put her thoughts into words Alejandro's arms tightened around her and his mouth sought hers. 'Let's not talk about Inocente any more,' he muttered thickly. '*Dios*, Tanya, how I have suffered today. Do not do this to me again.'

'You think I haven't suffered too?' She tried to pull away, but his arms tightened.

'*Querida*, I am sure you have, but I will make it up to you, I promise.' His mouth closed over hers, and instantly Tanya was lost. Whatever this man did, whatever he said, contact with him was always explosive. In this respect at least nothing had changed.

The kiss deepened, but when he tried to take their lovemaking further Tanya wrenched herself away. 'No, Alejandro, not tonight.' Not any night, in fact, not until she was very, very sure of his feelings.

His frown grew harsh. 'This is because of Inocente?'

Tanya nodded, but it was only partly true. She wanted to know where she stood before she continued any sort of intimate relationship; she wanted to know what he felt, what the future held in store for her.

He muttered beneath his breath. 'I am sorry this has happened, Tanya, and I am even more sorry that I cannot stay and put matters right between us, but I must get home to Manolo.' He looked angry at his commitment. 'I want you to promise me, Tanya, that tomorrow you will be here when I come. No more running away?'

'I promise,' she said quietly, almost uninterestedly.

His lips tightened. 'And if Inocente turns up again do not speak to her; send her away and let me deal with her. *Buenas noches, amor mío*. I am sorry you have been so troubled.

'*Buenas noches*, Alejandro.'

He did not kiss her again, for which Tanya was grateful, because she doubted whether she would have been able to stop herself responding, and when he had gone her mind was a maelstrom. She needed proof that he wanted more from her than her body, proof that his intentions were serious, and until that time came she had to hold him off, no matter how difficult she found it.

CHAPTER TEN

TO TANYA's relief the next few days were so hectic
that there was no time for intimacies, no time for in-
depth conversations. There was so much going on,
every day something different: the opening parade, the
comparsas show, the dancers, the fancy dress contest,
the songs of the *rondallas* — street musicians — the
murgas — groups of musical critics poking fun at local
dignitaries and politicians — the orchestral musical festival, and, of course, the grand procession.

Manolo came for that, and all Alejandro's brothers
and sisters and aunts and uncles and nephews and
nieces who were not taking part in the parade. Tanya
had learned that La Orotava's own *carnaval* was taking
place this week too, but because most members of
Alejandro's family lived nearer to Santa Cruz, it was
the custom for them all to come here.

It took four hours for the parade to pass by.
Alejandro found her a vantage point where she could
see everything clearly, and she waved enthusiastically
at Beatriz, looking beautiful and elegant in her silver
and purple costume.

Alejandro had even persuaded Tanya to paint her
face — her eyes were outlined dramatically, and glitter
and jewels stuck to her cheeks. Everyone entered into
the spirit of the *carnaval*, he told her.

The television cameras were there, beaming the
proceedings out live all over the Canaries and mainline
Spain, positioned high on a scaffold where they got the
best view, arc lights illuminating the parading men,
women and children when night fell. The locals were
there, the tourists with their cameras and camcorders;
everyone but everyone was at the *coso*.

142

It was vibrant, gaudy, magnificent, brash, smelly, crowded, frenetic. It was everything. Tanya had never seen a parade before on such a lavish scale. Refreshment kiosks did a roaring trade. Pampero rum and Cola was the traditional drink, Alejandro told her as he handed her a glass later on when the parade had finished and the street party began.

The words 'fast food' took on a new meaning when Tanya saw the speed with which stallholders made up hot-dogs and hamburgers. Then there were the stalls that sold sweets and popcorn and balloons. Everywhere was noisy and crowded and aggressive and gaudy. She loved it.

The fireworks display was something else too, and Manolo's face was a picture of wonder. Tropical salsa music beat out into the early hours. There were people dancing, drinking, eating, laughing, shouting, children crying, mothers soothing. Manolo kept going for much longer than Tanya expected, but finally Alejandro said it was time to take his son home.

Tanya did not want the day to end either; she had never enjoyed a party so much in her life. And although Alejandro had been fun these last few days he had left her strictly alone. Contrarily she resented it, her whole body constantly throbbing with need of him.

On Ash Wednesday it was the Burial of the Sardine — a ritual in which a huge papier mâché sardine filled with fireworks, was pulled through the streets, followed by lamenting women dressed in black. It was then dropped into the sea, and exploded. 'It's a traditional way of wishing good fishing for the coming year,' explained Alejandro when Tanya questioned him.

Afterwards there was a further fireworks display, and for another two days there were celebrations of one sort or another. And then it was all over — in Santa Cruz at least.

'Now is the time,' Alejandro told her, 'for other towns to have their own carnivals. It is unfortunate Orotava held theirs this week — it would have been an excuse for you to stay at my house — but if you want to go to any of the others?' There was a glint in his eye as he spoke, and Tanya felt her heartbeats quicken, her pulses race all out of time with themselves.

It was late and they were in his apartment, sitting lingering over a meal Tanya had cooked them, the first time they had spent any real time alone since Inocente had ruined things for her.

'I don't think I could stand the pace,' she said with a short laugh. 'I'm going back to Matilde's tomorrow to recover.' There was still something of an atmosphere between them; she still did not know what his true feelings for her were, so she intended to distance herself from him now that the *carnaval* was over. It was the perfect excuse. And if he was seriously interested, then it would be up to him to make a move.

'And what if I say I don't want you to go?'

Her heart quickened its beat, and she paused a moment before answering in case he had something further to add, but when he remained silent, she said, 'I'm going home to England in a few days. I want to see some more of my sister before then.'

Alejandro frowned in surprise. 'Your holiday is almost over? Tanya, that cannot be; you must stay longer.'

She shook her head. 'It's not possible; I have a job to go to and a house to look after. I must get back.' She hoped he would tell her to give up her job, to sell her house, and come to live with him here in Tenerife. She hoped he would ask her to marry him.

But all he said was, 'Then let us spend at least one more day together.'

Tanya felt a lump of disappointment well in her throat; she had her answer. One more day and it would be over. He did not love her; his feelings were, as she had guessed, purely physical. 'What good will one more day do?' she asked, hoping her voice would not give her away.

'I thought we could go out on my yacht. It's rarely free for my own personal use, so when it is I like to make the most of it. Will you come?'

Tanya was sorely tempted. It was an opportunity too good to miss, but would she be doing the right thing? You've spent the whole week with him; what does one more day matter? asked a little voice inside her. Nothing, she supposed, except that it would make parting all the harder, and except that she could be in danger of giving herself away. She had managed to distance herself from him these last few days, but being alone on his yacht would be very different from mixing with thousands of people at the *carnaval*.

'Is it such a difficult decision?' he asked softly, his dark eyes ever watchful on hers.

'I'm torn between loyalty to my sister and the thought of a day out at sea. I've never been on a yacht before.'

'Then you have no choice,' he urged insistently. 'Charlene will be at work in any case, and I promise to take you straight back to Matilde's afterwards.'

Tanya gave in reluctantly. 'Ok, I'll come.' The thought of it accelerated her heartbeats. It could be what they both needed, a day free of interruptions, away from other people. Maybe he would tell her how he felt; maybe this was his plan.

Tanya was ready when Alejandro came to pick her up the next morning. She wore white cotton trousers, rubber-soled shoes, and a navy and white striped jumper. In her bag she had put her bikini, sun-cream, sunglasses, a towel — and a jacket. She still hadn't got over how much cooler this northern tip of the island was.

He appraised her silently, nodding his approval. He had on a navy sweatshirt and jeans, and Tanya could not remember ever seeing him dressed so casually. Not that he looked less attractive; far from it. Already her pulses were racing, and she had high hopes for the outcome of today. She had spent most of the night worrying, but in the end had decided that only good could come out of it. She would relax and enjoy herself and let things take their natural course.

His yacht, named *Water Dancer*, was much bigger than she expected, and Tanya was very impressed. 'I love it,' she said excitedly. 'I love the name; I love everything about it.'

'I'm glad you approve,' he said solemnly.

'What do you want me to do?'

'Nothing, just stand around and look beautiful.' His tone was deep and sensual, and Tanya felt her adrenalin begin to flow.

He untied the boat, started the engine, and slowly and steadily steered her out of the harbour. Tanya watched him, admiring the ease with which he handled the vessel, and as they left Tenerife behind, as the island became smaller and smaller until it was no more than a dot on the horizon, her excitement grew. She felt confident that today she would find out exactly what Alejandro's feelings were.

'I had a word with Inocente,' he said, after they had been going for about an hour. Up until then they had spoken about nothing except the boat, the glorious weather, everything in fact except themselves. She had explored *Water Dancer*, admired the layout, the ultra-smart galley, the luxurious cabins, the sumptuous lounge, and now she was beside him again, watching his strong, capable hands on the wheel.

'What did she say?' Her heart skipped an uneasy beat. She did not want to talk about Inocente today; she wanted nothing to spoil this rare occasion.

'She admitted she had deliberately tried to break us up.'

'Did she really?' Tanya did not altogether believe

him. 'And did she also tell you how she'd found out that I wasn't seeing you on that particular morning?'

'From Cecilia, my daily housekeeper,' he said with a wry twist to his lips. 'Inocente came round to my house; the woman told her in all innocence.'

'I see, and why did she come round to your house when you were supposed to have finished with her?' It sounded to Tanya as though he had not done a very good job of it.

'She does not give up easily, unfortunately.'

'So it would seem,' she snapped. 'And there's also the fact that you said she had never been to your apartment when she told me she had. One of you is lying.'

'Tanya, *amor mío*, I can assure you she has not, not ever. She got that address also from Cecilia. The woman was particularly indiscreet. I have already spoken to her. And if it will put your mind at rest, I gave Inocente a piece of my mind also for telling such outrageous lies. I do not think she will be troubling us again.'

Tanya smiled weakly. Maybe not, but the damage was already done. There was still a thin thread of suspicion that would not go away.

They dropped anchor round about one o'clock, and Alejandro produced a bottle of champagne and a superb cold buffet lunch, and afterwards she put on her bikini and lay on the deck in the warm sunshine. Earlier it had been chilly, but now it was still and warm and she closed her eyes.

Alejandro changed into his swimming-trunks too and sat down beside her, and the next second she felt his hands on her legs, applying her sun-cream. 'It is far too easy to get burnt in this African sun,' he told her.

It was an excuse to touch her, and Tanya knew it, and she felt fire course through her limbs. When suddenly he stopped she opened her eyes and he was looking at her intently, desire darkening his eyes.

'Tanya, *querida*,' he said hoarsely, 'I can resist you no longer.' And his mouth came down on hers, hesitantly at first, until he met with no resistance, and then it was a kiss of mutual hunger.

They had both been building up to it all morning and, despite their talk about Inocente, neither could hold anything back. Tongues entwined; bodies pressed. Tanya's hands reached up into the thick blackness of his hair; his hands explored the curves of her body, disposing with indecent haste of her spotted bikini top, teasing her already erect nipples between thumb and forefinger.

Tanya arched her body into his, excitement running like quicksilver through her limbs. Any second now she expected his whispered words of love. This was the moment she had been waiting for.

'*Mi corazón*, Tanya mine.' His fingers trailed over the flatness of her stomach, inching inside the edge of her bikini bottom, easing it down over her hips, exploring, inciting, sending her soaring sky-high.

But when he began to take off his own swimming-trunks too she knew she had to stop him. Disappointment washed over her, engulfing her, saddening her, angering her. If this was all he wanted, then he could take a running jump. She was not his plaything; this wasn't the reason she had come out with him today. It was words of love she wanted, not the physical act.

'No, Alejandro.' She rolled away from and sat up, her hands around her knees, her whole body tense.

'No?' His voice sounded loud out here where all was still and quiet, save for the swishing of the waves against the side of his boat.

'No.'

He swore violently and jerked himself to his feet where he stood looking down at her, his face harshly critical. '*Maldito sea*! Tanya, I have waited patiently. I have waited for you to be ready, for you to make the first move, to give me some form of encouragement. I did not want to rush you. I thought this was the moment. It is obvious I was wrong; it is obvious I am wasting my time.' He gave a snort of anger and hurled himself towards the cabin.

Tanya closed her eyes, tears squeezing through her lids and rolling down her cheeks. This was it. It was all over; there was no hope left. Alejandro had proved that all he wanted was her body, an affair, a physical relationship. It was all he had ever wanted. He had no feelings for her, not real feelings, not like the ones she had for him.

Today had been a mistake; she ought to have gone back to Matilde's, as she had planned. Except that then she would have kept wondering and hoping, and now she knew that there was no hope. She shivered and rubbed her arms and wanted to go into the cabin to get her clothes, but because Alejandro was there she refrained.

Not until he came back out, fully dressed, and restarted the engine did she get to her feet. She glanced across at him, but his face was set, his eyes straight ahead, and she spun on her heel and marched inside.

Her hands were trembling as she pulled on her trousers and jumper, and her head was held high when she walked back out to the deck. She had been tempted, for a moment, to stay there out of sight, but that was the coward's way out. If he wanted to be offended because she wouldn't let him make love, then that was his bad luck, not hers. Why shouldn't she enjoy the rest of the voyage?

'Enjoy' was perhaps the wrong word. The atmosphere was so thick that it could be cut with a knife. 'I don't know why you're behaving like this,' she snapped, when she could bear the silence no longer. 'Surely I'm not the first woman to say no to you?' Or maybe she was; maybe that was what was annoying him.

His eyes were cold on hers. 'That isn't the issue,

Tanya; surely you know that? Surely you know what is wrong?'

She knew he didn't love her, but if it wasn't because she had rejected him that was making him so cold then she didn't know what was. But she had no intention of admitting her ignorance, and she lifted her shoulders in an indifferent shrug. 'So you're going to spoil the rest of the day because of it?'

His fingers clenched the wheel so tightly that his knuckles shone white. 'You make it sound as though it means nothing.'

'What is to be will be,' she said. 'You can't make things happen.'

'You're damn right you can't.' Her words seemed to anger him more and more, and the boat was going so fast that it seemed to be almost skimming the waves.

Maybe it would be best after all if she kept out of his way. She returned to the main cabin and sat on one of the grey velvet seats. To her relief he eased off the throttle slightly, and the journey back to Tenerife was accomplished in reasonable comfort — of the body if not the mind!

They reached the harbour and he steered the boat skilfully back into its berth. Tanya climbed off, not looking forward to the ride home. This was the end, apparently, of their relationship. His feelings had never been as great as hers, and now it was all over.

She wished that she had never let Charlene persuade her to come to Tenerife. In the nine years since she had first loved and lost Alejandro she had pushed him right out of her mind. Not completely — it was impossible ever to forget a person you had loved so deeply — but she had resigned herself to a life without him. . . and now all the old heartache had come back. There would be months and months spent thinking about him, wishing that things had been different.

Suddenly she remembered that she had left her bag on the deck where she had been standing as he tied up.

At the exact moment she turned she saw Alejandro pitch forward, try to save himself, and then hit the deck with a resounding thud. She had never run so quickly in her life, and her heart was thumping desperately when she scrambled on board. He made no move to get up.

'Alejandro.' Her voice rose shrilly. '*Alejandro*!' Panic began to set in. What if he was dead? She put her fingers to the side of his neck, feeling for his pulse. To her relief she found it. But he was still unconscious. She mustn't try to move him; she must get help. Off the boat again she jumped, and to her relief saw the harbour master. She ran up to him. 'Please, you must help. My friend's tripped and knocked himself out. He needs an ambulance.'

'*Ambulancia? Si.* I do it at once.'

The next few minutes were agonising. Alejandro was still unconscious when the ambulance arrived. They let her ride with him to the private clinic, and she waited while he was X-rayed and examined. He had apparently hit his head when he fell, and although there appeared to be no serious injury they could not be one hundred per cent sure until he regained consciousness. No one could tell her how long that would be.

Tanya had never felt so devastated in her life. She was finally allowed to see Alejandro when he was put in his hospital bed, and she could have cried when she saw how pale and still he looked. . .and it was all her fault. She had realised when she got back to the yacht that he must have caught his foot in the strap of her bag. By her own forgetfulness she had put his life in danger. How could she live with it if he died?

Crisógono, as the closest relative Tanya knew, was informed and he turned up at the clinic just as Tanya thought of leaving. 'Oh, Cris,' she cried, flinging herself into his arms. 'Please let him be all right.'

'My brother's tough.' He told her with a smile that

she knew was forced. 'We must all hope and pray, but I'm sure he'll pull through.'

'I hope so,' she whispered brokenly.

'How did it happen?'

She felt her face colouring as she told him about the bag, but he insisted that she must not blame herself. 'Alejandro should have looked where he was walking,' he said, but she could see the strain in his face.

'Manolo!' she exclaimed suddenly. 'Alejandro told me his nanny is off on a week's holiday. He was going to friends straight after school, and they're bringing him home at six. Someone must be there to tell him about his father, to stay with him. Oh, Cris, what are we going to do? Shall I go?' It was the very least she could do. 'Manolo likes me; he knows we were going out together today.' Goodness, what did you tell an eight-year-old child?

'I think that's a good idea,' said Crisógono. 'I'd like to stay here a while with Alejandro, just in case he regains consciousness, but I'll tell Beatriz when I get home and I've no doubt she'll come to see you.'

He found her the house key in Alejandro's trouser pocket and Tanya took a taxi to La Orotava, after first directing the driver to the apartment in Santa Cruz so that she could pick up her clothes; Cris said he would arrange to fetch Alejandro's car later. It felt strange entering the house by herself; she felt almost guilty. And as she walked through the rooms she could sense Alejandro, almost as though he were there with her.

She found the kitchen, a large room looking as though it had recently been modernised, and made herself a cup of coffee, but before she had taken even one sip of it she heard Manolo's excited voice. 'Papá, Papá, *donde estás*?'

The boy stopped short when he saw Tanya instead of his father, but he grinned easily. '*Hola*, Tanya.'

'Hello, Manolo,' she answered gravely.

'*Dónde está* Papá?' He looked around the kitchen

expectantly. 'Oh, I am sorry. I forget you do not speak Spanish. Where is Papá? I have a lot to tell him.'

'Manolo,' Tanya went down on one knee front of him and took his small hands into hers, wondering how on earth she was going to break the news. 'I am afraid your daddy is not here. He is poorly; he is—in hospital.'

Manolo's already large eyes widened considerably and his face grew pale. 'Papá is in hospital?' Tears began to well. 'But I want my *papá*. Tanya, I want him here. He must come home; I want him.'

'That is not possible, my darling.' She pulled him into her arms. 'He is not very well.'

'What is wrong with him? Papá is never sick, never.'

'He fell, Manolo. He fell and hurt his head, as you fall sometimes.'

'But I do not go to the hospital.'

'Because you are never badly hurt.'

'Papá is hurting a lot?'

'He is asleep at the moment.'

'I want to go to him.'

The tears were falling fast now, and Tanya produced a handkerchief, mopping his face, but no sooner had she dried one lot of tears than another instantly followed. 'Your daddy wouldn't know you were there,' she told him softly. 'Tomorrow, perhaps, you can go; he will be much better then.' She mentally crossed her fingers that she was right.

'Will you stay with me, Tanya?' He raised his little tear-stained face to hers.

'Of course, my darling. Of course I will.'

'All night?'

'Yes, Manolo.'

'Will you sleep with me?'

Tanya was not sure that his father would approve of that; he had brought his son up to be much older than his years.

'I'll sleep in the next room, and we'll leave the doors open.'

'And the light on?'

'Just a little one.'

'How did Papá fall? What was he doing?'

'He tripped and fell on his yacht. We had just come back. He banged his head.' Manolo was a sensible boy; she did not see why she should not tell him the truth.

'I hurt my head once. Papá bandaged it up. Does he have a bandage on?'

Tanya shook her head. 'No, he hasn't.'

The news seemed to reassure Manolo. He obviously thought it couldn't be too bad if he wasn't bandaged. 'I am hungry, Tanya.'

'Then you tell me what you would like and we'll do it together.'

Later, when Manolo was in bed, she telephoned Charlene to explain why she wouldn't be back.

'But it's not your place to look after his son,' said her sister resentfully. 'He has family; why can't they do it?'

'Because I want to. It's my fault he's in hospital; it's the very least I can do.'

'I think you're crazy.'

'You don't understand.'

'Don't forget you're flying home on Friday.'

'I won't. How's Juan? I saw him the other day.'

'Yes, he told me; he's fine. I'll explain about his cousin. Maybe he'll be able to organise someone else to look after Manolo.'

Tanya felt like screaming, and after a few more words with her sister she put down the phone. She ought to have known Charlene would not understand.

And then Beatriz came, flustered, anxious, concerned both about her brother-in-law and his son. 'This is terrible.' she said, hugging Tanya, and holding her for many long seconds. 'Poor Alejandro.'

'Have you been to the clinic?'

'Not yet. Cris, he tell me all about it.'

'Alejandro has not regained consciousness?'

'No.'

The two women went on talking and worrying, and Beatriz asked Tanya if she would continue to look after Manolo. 'We all have families of our own,' she explained. 'He could come to one of us, of course, but he would worry that his father might come home and he would not be here. He will be happier in his own home. It is unfortunate that his nanny is away.'

'I'll stay for as long as I'm needed,' said Tanya. Even if it meant extending her holiday she would stay. This was the man she loved. Looking after his son was the very least she could do, especially as the accident had been her fault.

The thought would not go away, keeping her awake all through the night, and when she heard Manolo call out she was at his side immediately.

He was dreaming, thrashing about in the bed, calling for his father. Tanya put a soothing hand on his forehead, murmuring softly, encouragingly, trying to relax and comfort him, having no idea whether she got through, but finally he lay still, his breathing deep and normal.

For the rest of the night Tanya sat in his room. She saw no point in going back to bed when she would not sleep. The armchair was deep and comfortable, and she imagined Manolo curled up in it with his father while he read him a story. She had always regretted that she and Peter had no children. If she'd had a little boy she would have wanted him to be like Manolo, polite and well-behaved, a genuine joy to be with and to take out anywhere.

The next thing she knew it was daylight and Manolo was tugging her arm. 'Wake up, Tanya, wake up. I want to go and see Papá.'

It took Tanya a second or two to realise where she was and what had happened, and when she did she hugged Manolo closely. This precious child was the son of the man she loved and he was worried about him, the same as she was. It was a bond they shared at this moment in time.

'I think your daddy would insist that you go to school. When you come out I will take you, I promise.'

'I don't want to go to school.' Tears began to roll down his cheeks again.

'Oh, Manolo, I know you don't. There are lots of things in life that we don't want to do, but we have to. Please be a brave boy for your daddy's sake.'

He buried his face in her chest and she let him cry, stroking his thick black hair, so like his father's, and in a minute or two he had pulled himself together. 'If you think it is what Papá would want me to do, then I will go.' He was trying very hard to be brave.

Tanya hugged him. 'You're a good boy, Manolo.

'And you will take me when I come out?'

'Yes, of course, I promise.'

'At lunchtime?'

Tanya shook her head. 'Oh, no, you must have your siesta. I will take you after you have finished for the day.' Cris had explained to her that his brother's housekeeper would be there to keep her eye on him. 'And now I think you should get washed and dressed while I see to your breakfast.'

She found out that Manolo normally went to school with a friend who lived near by, so after she had taken him there, Manolo explaining to the boy's mother what had happened, because the woman did not speak English, she took a taxi to the hospital.

She kept her fingers mentally crossed that Alejandro would have come out of his coma, hurrying down the ward, not bothering to ask whether it would be all right; no one would have stopped her anyway. When she saw the empty bed, every vestige of colour drained from Tanya's face, Oh, no, please, no. There was some mistake. She was in the wrong ward; this couldn't have happened. Oh, please, God, no. 'No!' The word came out in a thin wail.

CHAPTER ELEVEN

THE next thing Tanya knew she was sitting on the bed, surrounded by nurses, a glass of water being pushed into her hand. 'Alejandro,' she managed to gasp. 'What has happened to him?'

There was much gesticulating and talking, but Tanya did not know what they were saying. 'English,' she said. 'Please speak in English.' But no one spoke her language and she began to feel desperate, until another nurse, seeing the commotion, stopped to see what was going on, and to Tanya's relief he spoke English.

'Where is Alejandro Vázquez?' she asked. 'He was in this bed last night.'

After a brief discussion with the nurses he told her that Alejandro had been moved earlier that morning to a clinic in Santa Cruz.

Intense relief washed over her.

'His brother organised it,' went on the doctor. 'He did not tell you?'

Tanya shook her head. 'I was so afraid that Alejandro. . .' Her voice was too choked to speak her thoughts.

'I will give you the address,' said the doctor kindly. 'This man is your husband?' He had noticed the ring on her finger.

'No, my—er—friend. I was with him when the accident happened.'

'I see; I understand your concern. You have a car?'

'No.'

'Then I will get someone to order you a taxi. Come, come with me.'

At the clinic Tanya was taken to Alejandro's room. She had no idea what to expect and was deeply distressed when she saw that he was still unconscious. There were tubes and wires monitoring his every breath. He did not look ill or pale or anything like that, he looked just as though he were naturally asleep, and when Tanya was left alone she took his hand in hers.

'Oh, Alejandro, please get better. I love you so much. I can't bear the thought that you're hurt, and all because of my stupidity in forgetting my bag. If we hadn't argued it wouldn't have happened. I should never have stopped you making love to me. I love you desperately. Oh, my darling, please speak, please open your eyes, *please*.' But there was nothing, no response, not even the flicker of an eyelid.

She continued to talk to him, to tell him her inner-most feelings, to hold his hand, to stroke it, to look at him, to study every line on his face. He was so handsome, so beautiful, so everything. She touched his face, his eyelids, his nose, his mouth, his infinitely kissable lips. She leaned forward and pressed her lips to his. 'I love you, Alejandro. I love you with all my heart.' Her tears fell on his cheeks and she wiped them away with a gentle finger.

And then a noise behind made her turn, and there was Beatriz, her own eyes moist. Tanya wondered how long she had stood there, but she did not feel embarrassed.

'You found him, I see. I telephoned to tell you he had been moved, but no answer. I not think you come this early.'

'I took Manolo to his friend's and then went straight to the hospital,' Tanya told her. 'I don't mind telling you I thought the worst when I saw his bed empty.'

'I am sorry you were worried,' said Beatriz, her hand coming over Tanya's. 'We thought it better to have him nearer home. Alejandro, he will pull through, I am sure. He is strong. He will be all right. How is Manolo?'

'He wanted to come,' said Tanya with a wry smile.

'He wanted to see his father last night. I've promised he can see him when he finishes school.'

'What have you told him?'

'I told him about the accident, but I just said he was asleep last night. I haven't told him that he hasn't woken at all.'

Beatriz nodded. 'He adores Alejandro. I am so proud of the way he has brought the boy up.'

'He does him credit,' agreed Tanya.

'*Sí*, very much so.' She glanced fondly at her brother-in-law. 'I do not know any other man who would do this for a boy who was not his own.'

Tanya looked sharply at Beatriz. 'What do you —'

Her question was cut off as a nurse hurried into the ward, followed closely by a man in a white coat who she presumed was the doctor.

'We had better get out,' said Beatriz, 'and I must go. I came to check you had found Alejandro, and to see how he was, of course. I'll be back later. You will still be here?'

'Yes,' agreed Tanya. 'I shall stay all day if they'll let me.'

But that was not possible, she was told afterwards. She ought not to be here now. She could come back later in the morning and then again this afternoon.

In the taxi Tanya's thoughts were in chaos. What had Beatriz meant when she said Manolo wasn't Alejandro's? If he wasn't Alejandro's son, then whose boy was he? Perhaps he was adopted. Was that what she had meant? Perhaps Juanita hadn't been able to have children. But why hadn't Alejandro told her? On the other hand, why should he? He clearly regarded Manolo as his own, and probably saw no reason to tell anyone that he wasn't actually his own flesh and blood.

Back at Alejandro's house Tanya met his house-keeper, who had no idea that her employer was in hospital. To begin with she had been suspicious of this strange girl who had come walking into the house, but once Tanya explained what had happened—with mime and careful use of words, because she also could speak no English—she accepted her. Cecilia was very distressed when she learned what had happened.

Alejandro's car had turned up in her absence, and Tanya decided to use it to go back and forth to the hospital. It was costing her a small fortune in taxi fares. She wished there were some change in him; she wished he would come round. She talked and talked, pouring out her heart and soul, but all to no avail.

Cris came, and other brothers and sisters of Alejandro, all looking suitably solemn, and Tanya felt sure they must be blaming her. She had told Crisógono that it was her bag he had fallen over, and she felt sure he must have passed the word on. Even the fact that they were friendly towards her made no difference to her guilt.

When Manolo arrived home from school his first words were that he wanted to visit his father, and, true to her promise, Tanya took him. She prayed that Alejandro would be awake, but he wasn't. Manolo stood and looked with great interest at all the tubes and instruments, but he did not say anything. He seemed to take for granted the fact that when you were ill in hospital they did all sorts of things to you.

'Papá doesn't look poorly,' he whispered to Tanya.

'No, he doesn't,' she agreed. 'But he's hurting inside, and that's why he's sleeping all the time.'

'He does not feel the hurt when he is asleep?'

'That's right, Manolo. You can talk to him if you like; he might hear you.'

'Like as if it is a dream?' he asked, his eyes wide.

Tanya nodded.

'I dreamt about Papá last night.'

'Yes, I know, I heard you.'

'I cried; I was frightened. I thought Papá was going to die.'

'No, Manolo.' Tanya gathered him to her. 'Your

papá is going to get well. You tell him now that he must get better; tell him you want him home.'

They spent an hour at the hospital, and at the end of it she could see that Manolo was beginning to get agitated. Then Beatriz and Crisógono came again with their two children, and he was happy when he had someone his own age to talk to. He ran off with his cousins, and Tanya said to Cris, 'How long do you think he will be like this?'

Cris shook his head sadly. 'I do not know; the doctors do not know either. We have to be patient.'

Being patient was the hardest thing Tanya had ever had to do. She slept that night, but only because her body insisted, and the next day she was at the clinic as soon as it was allowed. Manolo came with her again after school, and Tanya began to worry that his father's continuing sleep might have some detrimental effect on him.

'Why doesn't Papá wake up?' he kept asking, and Tanya had to tell him that it was because of his illness. 'But he can hear us talking,' she assured him.

'I could sing to him,' said Manolo hopefully. 'Papá likes to me to sing.'

'That's a wonderful idea,' she agreed at once. 'I'd like to hear you sing as well.'

And so, in a clear, high voice, without any sign of self-consciousness, Manolo began to sing. Tanya had no idea what it was, because he sang in his native language, but it sounded very cheerful, and as she watched Alejandro she thought she saw his eyelids flicker, and a tiny movement of his fingers. Manolo did too, because he halted and then went on with renewed vigour, and this time Alejandro definitely showed signs of hearing his son's voice.

It was with a struggle that his eyes eventually opened, as though his lids were glued together and he was having to prise them apart. 'Papá! Papá!' Manolo threw himself at his father before Tanya could restrain him, and Alejandro's arms came about his son.

Tanya felt tears well, and wondered whether she ought to go out the room. Alejandro would not want her here, not after their argument. She was the very last person he would wish to speak to.

But already Alejandro' s eyes were on her. At first he frowned, as if trying to recollect what had happened, and then he let go of his son and held out his hand to Tanya. 'Come here,' he said faintly.

But at that moment a nurse came into the room to make one of her routine checks, and, upon seeing Alejandro conscious, she let out a cry of pleasure. 'It is good; it is good. I will fetch the doctor.'

Hanging back then, in case the doctor came immediately Tanya was surprised when Alejandro said more strongly, 'Tanya, I want to hold you.'

With a faint smile she joined Manolo, and the two of them held on to him for a few poignant moments. Perhaps he hadn't yet remembered their argument, she thought, clinging to these few precious moments. And then the doctor came and they were ushered out and more tests and examinations were made over the next hour or so, until finally the medical staff pronounced they could find nothing wrong. 'But we will keep him in for a few days' observation,' the doctor told her.

Beatriz and Crisógono and their children came after that and Tanya left, feeling that she was in the way. Beatriz promised to bring Manolo home.

Tomorrow was the day she should be flying back to England, and that evening Charlene phoned her. 'I'm not going,' said Tanya at once, 'not until Alejandro's out of hospital. Manolo needs me. I've already cancelled my flight.'

'You're a fool. What if you lose your job?'

'No, I won't. I've telephoned John Drake and explained the position. He's going to keep the temp on until I get back.'

Charlene grumbled some more, but Tanya would not change her mind, and in bed that night she wondered if she was doing the right thing. She had not had a chance to tell Alejandro that she was looking after his son, though she had no doubt that Beatriz had done so. Would he appreciate it, or would he be angry and say she was pushing her nose in where it was not wanted?

Because she was not sure of the reception she would get Tanya almost did not go to visit him the next morning, until Manolo asked her to tell his daddy he would visit him after school; then she knew she had to go, for his son's sake. Manolo had clung to her these last few days. It was amazing how easily he had accepted her. They had built up a rapport that would be difficult to break, and she hoped the boy would not be too upset when she went back to England.

She would be upset herself, there was no doubt about it. Leaving Alejandro would be hard, devastating in fact, and it would be very difficult to carry on her life as though he had not happened. Though she knew she must. This had been just another interlude, exciting while it lasted but destined for failure.

When she got to the hospital, Alejandro, wearing a pair of deep blue Paisley pyjamas, was sitting in a chair near the wide-open window. He turned when he heard her footsteps, and Tanya held her breath, wondering what sort of reception she would get. He needed a shave; three days of growth had darkened his chin. 'Designer stubble', they called it, and actually it suited him; he would look very handsome with a beard, she thought. Not that he didn't already. His dark good looks had attracted her right from the very beginning, from the day she had seen him at her friend's wedding. Her heart had quickened its beats then, and it did the same now.

'Tanya.' His smile was welcoming but wary.

'Hello, Alejandro, how are you feeling?' She went

up to him, but not too close, because she knew if she did so she would want to throw herself into his arms.

'I'm anxious to get out of here,' he grumbled. 'I don't see why I can't leave now. I'm perfectly fit.'

'They need to make sure there are no after-effects, nothing they've missed.' She twisted her fingers uneasily. 'It was my fault you fell. If I hadn't forgotten my bag it wouldn't have been lying around. I'm sorry.'

'Hell, don't apologise. I should have looked where I was going. I was so damn mad at you, but I've done a lot of thinking since I came round. It was wrong of me to be angry simply because you said no. Will you ever forgive me?'

Tanya was startled by his apology, startled but pleased. 'I already have,' she said softly. 'I've done a lot of thinking too, Alejandro. I should never have let you kiss me when I knew I'd put a stop to it if you went too far.'

He looked as though he agreed. 'What I can't understand, Tanya, is that only two weeks ago we spent a wonderful night together, and now you're virtually holding me at arm's length. Why is that?'

Tanya drew in a deep breath and avoided looking at him. 'It was a mistake.'

'A mistake?' He frowned. 'Some mistake when you actively enjoyed it. And don't say you didn't, because no woman can act like that.'

'I did enjoy it,' she said with a rueful grimace, 'but it is something I have no intention of repeating.'

'Ever?' His dark eyes were watchful on hers.

Tanya drew in a deep breath and exhaled it slowly. 'If the circumstances were right I might,' she ventured, choosing her words carefully.

'And what would those circumstances be?' He pushed himself up from his chair and came to stand beside her, not touching, but close enough for her to feel the utter maleness of him, close enough to drive her insane.

She closed her eyes, and her voice was no more than a husky whisper. 'Mutual love. A one-sided affair is worse than no affair at all.'

'I agree,' he said to her surprise. 'Loving someone who doesn't love you can be torture.'

Tanya looked at him in astonishment. He knew! Oh, lord, he knew! Had Beatriz told him? Or had he guessed? Had she given herself away? She must change the subject quickly now, before it become too embarrassing. Inching away from him, she made a show of smelling the red roses that stood on his bedside table. Flowers for a man! She did not know who had sent them, but could only guess that it was Inocente. Her fingers curled.

As if he too had had enough of talking about themselves he said gruffly, 'I want to thank you for looking after Manolo. Things are bit hazy in my mind, but isn't it today you should be flying home?'

Tanya inclined her head. 'I cancelled it. I'll go once you're fit and well. Manolo asked me to tell you that he'll be in to see you when he comes out of school. He's been every day, talking to you, singing, praying. He loves you totally. Why didn't you tell me that he wasn't your real son?'

Alejandro looked at her sharply, and as if the surprise of her knowing was too great for him he sat down again. 'Who told you that?'

'Beatriz let it slip.' Tanya perched herself on the edge of the bed. 'She was admiring you. He really does you credit, Alejandro. Is he adopted?'

'No, not exactly.'

Tanya frowned. 'Then I don't understand. I presumed Juanita couldn't have children so you adopted.'

'Beatriz didn't tell you the circumstances?'

'No.'

He sighed heavily. 'It's quite a story.'

'If you're not up to it. . .' she said at once, half rising to leave.

He stayed her with his hand. 'I'd like you to know—if you really want to hear, that is.'

'I do,' she whispered. She wanted to hear anything to do with this man.

'It all began the day I wrote to Juanita telling her I'd fallen in love with you.'

He had actually told Juanita he loved her? Tanya was not convinced she could accept that. Maybe he had written to the girl, but surely not to say that he loved her? If he had loved her he would never have left England so suddenly.

'She was terribly distressed, because she had always thought that one day we would get married. Oh, we'd talked about it when we were young, I admit, but as I got older my feelings changed. I thought I'd made it clear to her, but obviously not, because on the rebound she went out with some other guy. He got her pregnant and then didn't want to know about it. When I got back here she was on the verge of suicide.'

'So you married her after all?'

Alejandro nodded.

He had certainly wasted no time, thought Tanya. One argument they'd had, and he'd married his childhood sweetheart. She admired his selflessness; it made her see him in a whole new light. She hadn't realised he had such a caring side to him. But—would he have done it if he hadn't genuinely loved Juanita? That was the crucial question.

'And when she died you brought up Manolo as your own? That was very generous of you.' And further proof that he had loved Juanita. Why else would he want to bring up someone else's child?

'I could do no less. Manolo and I had grown very close.'

'He always called you Papá?'

'Yes.'

'Does he know the truth?'

'No, although one day I expect I shall tell him.'

'Juanita's death must have been very traumatic for you.' She remembered when Peter died she had been inconsolable.

'Juanita was a very dear friend.'

'You are still claiming you did not love her?'

His brows lifted. 'It is the truth, Tanya.'

Tanya eyed him in bewilderment. 'You did that—married a woman you did not love, simply to give her respectability?'

'More than that: a shoulder to lean on, a friend in time of need, a companion.'

Tanya wished she could believe him. 'But she still loved you?'

He heaved a sigh. 'I guess so.'

Tanya wanted to ask whether he had ever made love to her; but it was too personal a question. She guessed he had; no man could live with a woman for six years and remain celibate. Unless of course he had married her on the understanding that he was free to indulge in other relationships. It was a saddening thought.

'And now you are still looking after Manolo, even though you don't have to.' What a large heart this man had. A pity none of it was extended towards her. 'Didn't Juanita have any family who could have taken him in?'

'No one knew in her family that he wasn't mine. Beatriz is the only one who knows, because Juanita used to be a friend of hers. I trusted her to tell no one.'

'You mustn't blame her,' said Tanya at once. 'She was upset; she spoke without thinking. She probably thought you'd already told me. You're a remarkable man, Alejandro. You amaze me, in fact.'

'I did what I wanted to do. I love Manolo as much as if he were my own. In fact I regard him as mine.'

'He's certainly a fine boy.'

'You get on well with him?'

Tanya nodded. 'He seems to have taken to me. I hope you didn't think I was being frightfully cheeky, staying at your house. Cris seemed to think it would be best.

'I'm glad you did.' His voice dropped an octave. 'I like the thought of you in my house. Did you like sleeping there?'

'Yes,' she said huskily, her pulses beginning a stampede. It was incredible the way he could set her on fire with just the tone of his voice.

'Did you think of me a little?' His brown eyes were narrowed and watchful.

'More than a little,' she confessed. 'I was desperately worried.'

That wasn't the answer he wanted, and it showed in his eyes. 'You were worried because you felt the accident was your fault? Or was there another reason?'

Tanya closed her eyes. Did she tell him? Could she risk declaring her love at the cost of being spurned?

'Tanya?' He had risen without her being aware of it and was now standing in front of her. 'Tanya, I need to know what your real feelings are.'

'My feelings have never changed from the moment I first met you,' she said huskily, still not looking at him, studying her hands instead.

She heard his swiftly indrawn breath. 'So it's never been anything more than a physical attraction—and now you're fighting it because your conscience tells you it's wrong.'

'*No!*' Her head shot up in quick denial.

'No?' He frowned. 'Then what do you feel?'

'Damn you, Alejandro,' she cried, 'why are you putting me through this? What's the point when we both know what your feelings are?'

'When a man loves a woman as much as I love you he likes to know where he stands,' he said quietly.

Tanya felt her mouth drop open. She had not heard him right; she couldn't have. Alejandro did not love her. He wanted no more from her than a sexual relationship; it was all he had ever wanted.

'You look surprised.' He sat down on the bed beside her, taking her hands into his own.

'Don't play games with me, Alejandro.'

'*Mi corazón*, I would never do that.' He lifted her hands to his mouth, kissing her fingers, stroking them. 'You see, like yours, *my* feelings have never changed. I hoped, *amor mío*, that you would one day love me too. It saddens me that this will never be.'

Tanya felt a deep joy well up from the pit of her stomach, spreading and growing until it engulfed her whole body. *Alejandro loved her!* The impossible had happened — and if what he said was true he had loved her all along. Yet why had he never said? Why had he let her think his feelings went no deeper than a surface attraction? 'I didn't know that you loved me,' she said so softly that he only just caught her words.

'Tanya, Tanya, how can that be? Haven't I shown by my actions, by my need of you, by every word I've said, that I love you?'

'You never put it into words,' she reproached quietly.

'Did I have to? My sweet, sweet girl, I thought my body said it all. Are you telling me that you never knew?'

She gave an almost imperceptible nod.

With a groan he gathered her to him, and for the very first time Tanya felt his love flow into her. She knew happiness such as she had never known before. She lifted her face towards his, expecting him to kiss her, disappointed when he did no more than brush his lips against her forehead.

Very gently he put her from him. 'But as you said earlier, for one person to love is worse than not loving at all.'

Now she could tell him; now she could open her heart without fear of making a fool of herself. Her eyes shone as she looked at him; her whole body sang. 'Alejandro, it is not one-sided.'

There was a sudden stillness about him, and his dark handsome eyes looked at her at first in wonder and then in growing disbelief.

'I love you too, Alejandro,' she said huskily.

He frowned. 'Is this a sudden decision?'

'Goodness, no,' she replied, shaking her head vigorously. 'I have always loved you, from the very moment we first met.'

'I want to believe you,' he said slowly. 'I want desperately to believe you, but how can it be when you turned your back on me nine years ago, when you disappeared out of my life as though you had gone off the face of the earth? And how can it be when you do not let me make love to you? No, Tanya, I do not believe you.' He got up suddenly and went over to the window, staring out at the gardens with their brilliant exotic flowers.

Tanya felt sudden bewilderment. How could he not believe her? What did she have to do to prove it? She had accepted his word; why did he not accept hers? She went over to him and touched his shoulders, and was surprised at how tense he was. 'Alejandro, it is true. I do love you. Please, you must believe me.'

He turned and his eyes were shuttered, as though he had pulled a mask down over his emotions. 'I am sorry; I cannot believe you. You are mistaking a chemical attraction for love, that is all, all it has ever been.'

'No, Alejandro, no. I *do* love you. I do.' She put her arms around him and pressed her lips to his, but it was like kissing a statue, and she stepped back in utter confusion.

'I think you should leave.' His voice was dead, lifeless, and she could not believe he was doing this to her.

'But Alejandro. . .' Her voice trailed off as to her dismay a nurse came into the room, followed by the doctor doing his daily rounds. Of all the inopportune moments. She gave him one last pleading glance as she left, but he was not even looking at her.

She stood outside for several long minutes, trying to decide whether to wait or leave the hospital altogether. What point was there in protesting her love when he had made up his mind? She kept shaking her head. It was unreal the way he had reacted. She would have thought that when he discovered their mutual love he would be overjoyed. Exactly why didn't he believe her?

Because she had walked out on him, he had said. That was a laugh for a start; *he* was the one who had left England. And because she wouldn't let him make love to her. Again, another inexcusable statement. He was out of his mind. The accident had done more to him than anyone realised. She would go; there was no point in continuing their conversation while he was so adamant. She would give him time to think, hopefully to accept the fact that she was telling the truth. Lord, it didn't bear thinking about. They had both admitted their love, and yet she was still as far away from him as ever.

CHAPTER TWELVE

WHEN Manolo came home from school he was eager to go and see his father, but Tanya insisted that he have something to eat first. This, she had discovered via Alejandro's housekeeper, was his normal routine, but she had let it slide while his father was in hospital, giving him a piece of fruit to keep him going until his meal when they got home.

Today, though, she wanted to put off the moment when she went back. Not that there would be any time for conversation — Manolo always monopolised his father, and usually other members of the family came too. It was generally only in the mornings that Tanya had Alejandro to herself.

Her plan did not really work, because Manolo wolfed down his sandwich and orange juice and pronounced himself ready in three minutes flat, and they were at the hospital at their usual time. To Tanya's intense relief Beatriz was already there, welcoming her warmly, and not seeming to notice the tension between her and Alejandro.

When visiting finished at seven Tanya had still not spoken to him privately, and as he let her go with a faint, regretful smile Tanya did not know whether she would be welcome again.

Outside Beatriz had a quiet word with her. 'I thought Alejandro seemed a little subdued. Do you know why?'

'I didn't notice,' lied Tanya, shaking her head. Not for anything was she prepared to disclose their earlier conversation.

'I hope he is not suffering in silence. I hope there is nothing wrong that he isn't telling us.'

'I shouldn't think so.' said Tanya.

'Please ask when you see him tomorrow. I know he will talk to you.'

Tanya grimaced. 'He doesn't tell me everything, Beatriz.'

'Then you must insist. If not I will see the doctor.'

Tanya spent an almost sleepless night. It was impossible to accept that now she had discovered Alejandro loved her he would not believe that she loved him. There must be some way she could make him see the truth, but how, if words alone would not do it?

She was no nearer a solution when she got up the next morning, and once she had taken Manolo to his friend's home she could not make up her mind whether to go to the hospital or not. She went back to the house, and was still debating when Cecilia came. The woman looked pleased to see her still there, pushing a carefully wrapped parcel into her hand. 'Alejandro, you give?' Tanya's decision was made for her.

It was with some trepidation that Tanya walked into Alejandro's ward. Today he was not sitting; he was pacing the room. He looked pale, and was not as well as yesterday, although his jaw was freshly shaven and he had on a clean pair of pyjamas.

'*Buenos días*,' Tanya.' It was a curt, almost uninterested greeting.

'*Buenos días*,' she replied quietly, swallowing the lump which had risen in her throat. She loved this man so much that it crucified her to be treated so distantly. How could he do it when he had confessed he loved her? 'Your housekeeper's sent this for you.' She handed him the parcel, which was obviously a book, careful not to let their fingers touch. Contact would be both explosive and disastrous; already she was brimming over with conflicting emotions.

'Thank you.' He put it on the windowsill, ready to be opened later, and when he said nothing further Tanya turned to leave. She had reached the doorway before he spoke. 'The doctor says I can go home tomorrow.'

She suddenly felt as though a heavy weight were sitting in the bottom of her stomach. Once he was home she would no longer be needed. It would be the end. She would go back to England and never see Alejandro again. She felt tears welling, and desperately tried to stop them. 'That's good news.' Lord, was that thin, wavery sound her own voice?

'You don't look particularly elated. I thought you'd be pleased. You can go home now without having to pretend any more.'

'Pretend?' she asked, shocked. 'My love for you is not pretence, Alejandro, nor is it purely physical. I don't know how you can think that.'

'I think maybe you do not even know that you are pretending. I think you are deceived by your feelings. I think you are mistaking desire for real emotions.'

'Damn you, Alejandro.' Tanya glared at him furiously. He was out of his mind; he had to be. The accident had affected his brain. But if that was the way he wanted to play it she wasn't going to beg and plead. She would pack her bags and go the moment he was discharged, and if he truly loved her he would come after her. If he didn't. . . She did not dare think about that.

She swung around on her heel without saying any more, hoping against hope that he would call her back as she marched down the corridor, but her footsteps echoed alone.

She did not go back to the house straight away, going down to the harbour instead and standing watching the ships coming and going. When she did finally return Cecilia had left and she went up to her room to pack her case. One more night she would stay, then the second he set foot inside tomorrow she would be gone. If he couldn't believe her, then he wasn't worth loving.

She sat forlornly outside in the courtyard, listening to the bird-song, looking up at the palms reaching as high as the building. Usually she loved the quiet serenity, but today her mind was in too much turmoil to feel anything but distress.

She could have been happy here with Alejandro, with Manolo, with their own children. Now she realised it had never been anything more than a pipe-dream. She and Alejandro were not destined for each other.

It was a long day. When Manolo came home she told him that she was not feeling well and could not take him to the hospital.

'But I want to see Papá,' he protested.

'Your daddy is coming home tomorrow,' she told him.

'He is?'

Tanya nodded.

Manolo's face broke into a big smile. 'I am so happy. I have missed my *papá*.'

There was no doubt, she thought, of the love this child had for the man who had brought him up as his own. Alejandro's love, too, for Manolo was undeniable. There was some good in him somewhere, even though at times she found it very hard to find.

She wondered what Inocente thought of it all; whether she would be willing to marry Alejandro and accept Manolo as well. And what did Manolo think of Inocente? Would he accept her as a mother? Would Alejandro marry Inocente? It was very possible. Even though he had professed to love her, he had married Juanita, so what was to say he wouldn't do it a second time? Lord, how she hurt inside.

Not surprisingly, Tanya had a terrible night, tossing and turning, worrying and wondering, crying, despairing, telling herself not to be stupid, getting up and walking about the room, making herself a hot drink, going back to bed, still not sleeping. Damn Alejandro, she kept telling herself, damn the man. He wasn't worth loving; he wasn't worth all this heartache.

She fell asleep as dawn broke, and was woken by Manolo jumping on her bed. 'Wake up, Tanya, wake up. What time is Papá coming? I do not have to go to school today, do I?' He was so excited that Tanya hadn't the heart to say yes.

'Of course you don't, my darling. It's the weekend.' In any case, it would probably be better if Manolo was here. She would be able to make her escape while the two of them were greeting each other. Manolo definitely wouldn't leave his father alone, and Alejandro would be pleased to see his so-called son too.

All day they waited. Cecilia came and went. Manolo began to get fretful 'I want my *papá*. Why doesn't he come, Tanya? Is he hurting again?'

Tanya was worried too, though she tried not to show it. 'Of course not. I expect he's waiting for the doctor to say he can come. The doctors are very busy. They have a lot of other people to look at.'

'I want to go to him,' sobbed Manolo, tears welling in his big brown eyes.

Tanya took him into her arms. 'He'll be here any minute now, I assure you.' She rocked him as though he were a baby, murmuring words of comfort, and, curled up in a corner of the settee, they both went to sleep.

'Papá, Papá.'

Tanya was woken by Manolo's excited cry. He leapt up and straight into Alejandro's waiting arms. How she wished that she could have greeted Alejandro so eagerly herself, so warmly, so lovingly. She was almost jealous of Manolo. And her time had come to leave. It was going to be the biggest wrench of her life.

Quietly she slipped out of the room. Neither saw her go. Upstairs she picked up her suitcase and took one last look around. She had grown to love this old house, could have been completely happy living here, looking after it for Alejandro. She had thought about it a lot, had entertained such high hopes, until he had dashed them to the ground like a leaf in a storm, taken her heart and tossed it mercilessly away.

When she finally turned he was standing in the doorway. 'What are you doing?' he asked gruffly.

'What does it look like?' she retorted. 'I'm leaving. There's no place for me here any more.' She did not realise how despairing she sounded.

'I don't want you to go.'

Tanya turned surprised eyes on Alejandro's face. He was deadly serious, no hint of a smile, nothing to say, Tanya, I've made a mistake; I know you love me, and I want us to be together for always. Nothing like that, but nevertheless he was serious.

'Why?' She mouthed the word without any actual sound coming out.

'Because — because I — I need you.'

'You're prepared to let me stay on here even though you think I don't love you?'

'We both want you to stay.' Manolo appeared from behind his father.

Tanya suddenly knew why Alejandro had asked her. It was for his son's sake; Manolo did not want her to go. But it would be too much of a strain living under the same roof as Alejandro while not sharing his bed. She could not do it.

She shook her head. 'I'm sorry, Manolo, but I have to go home to England. I have a job and a house. . .' And she was saying the same things she had said to his father.

'But I love you, Tanya,' wailed the boy, and, 'Papá loves you too, don't you Papá?'

Alejandro put his hand on Manolo's shoulder. 'The point is, Tanya does not love us. We cannot force her to stay.'

'Tanya does love me,' cried Manolo. 'I know she does; she told me so.'

Tanya remembered; she had been comforting him
yesterday when he couldn't go to visit his father, and
she had hugged him close and said, 'Oh, Manolo, I
love you so much.'

'And she loves you too, Papá, I am sure. Don't you,
Tanya?' The boy looked at her imploringly.

Tanya nodded slowly, 'Yes, Manolo, I love your
papá.'

'Manolo, I think you should leave the room.'
Alejandro's voice was hoarse. 'I want to talk to Tanya
alone.'

'You are going to ask her to stay?'

Alejandro inclined his head.

Manolo smiled. 'Then I will go. But please don't be
long. I have waited all day for you, Papá.'

When he had gone Alejandro stepped into the room
and closed the door behind him. His eyes searched her
face. 'Would you lie to my son, Tanya?'

'Of course not.' Her eyes never wavered from his.
Something told her that this was the testing time. Her
heart beat louder.

'You told Manolo you loved me.'

'I also told *you* that I loved you.'

'It is the truth?'

'The choice is yours whether you believe me or not.'
She was not going to beg him to accept her word.

His eyes flickered uncertainly. 'I want to believe you,
Tanya.'

He had already said that to her.

'But I was hurt once before, I thought you loved me
nine years ago and then——' he made a sound like air
escaping from a balloon '—it was all over. You walked
out of my life and disappeared without a trace.'

'We have already had this conversation,' railed
Tanya. 'And I was not the one who did the walking
out. OK, we argued, and I left, but I came after you—
and what did I find? That you'd gone back to Tenerife.

And that was it, the end, no further word from you. So how the hell can you say that *I* walked out on you?'

Alejandro frowned, a deep frown that cut into his forehead and pulled his brows together until they almost looked like one line across his face. 'You came after me?'

'That's right.'

'Who did you speak to? Were you given no message?'

'Hell, I don't know who I spoke to; everyone at the hotel, I think. And no, I wasn't given a message. All I was told was that you had gone home to Tenerife.' She saw the changing expressions on his face. 'Are you saying that you left a note for me?'

'Not a note, no; it was verbal. I didn't have time for writing letters. My father was dying; I had to get home, and quickly. But I tried to get in touch with you later. . . Oh I don't know how long—a couple of weeks, or more, maybe. My father had died before I even got here, and his affairs were in such a mess there was much to do; he had left no will, nothing. But I thought you would have my message and understand. I thought you would wait for me.'

'I got no message,' she said, shaking her head, but hope suddenly riding high in her heart, 'and when I found you missing I was devastated. When my sister was offered a job in Sheffield I went with her. I could see no point in staying around Birmingham any longer. There were too many memories.'

He shook his head, his eyes full of pain. 'I tried to find you. I rang everyone I could think of. I even came back over to England, but you had disappeared without trace. I assumed you did not want me to find you.'

Tanya shuddered. If only she had known. 'So you married Juanita?' she asked quietly.

He nodded.

Tanya sighed, and they came together of mutual accord. His arms crushed her against him; his mouth found hers. Time stood still. Hearts throbbed, bodies pulsed, and Tanya felt as though she were being lifted to another planet. Life had turned full circle and she was back in the arms of the man she loved. And what was more, he loved her. Her happiness was complete.

'How much did you love Peter?' he asked when they finally drew apart. There was a faint frown on his brow, and he had obviously been thinking about this man who had been her husband.

'Not as much as I love you.' She looked at him, her eyes shining with honesty. 'We were happy enough together, but there was none of the magic I feel with you.'

'I'm glad,' he said huskily, 'because what I feel for you is very special too. When I came round in the hospital and saw you standing there I thought I was dreaming. After you'd rejected me on the yacht I really thought it was all over. Why did you do it?'

'Why did I reject you?' Her smile was wry. 'Because I thought all you were after was my body, and I couldn't handle that any longer. You'll never know how hard it was.'

'It looks as though we both made the same mistake.'

Tanya nodded sadly. 'Why didn't you ever mention that you'd tried to get in touch with me?'

He grimaced. 'Believe me, I wanted to, many times, but usually when things were running smoothly between us, and then I'd be afraid of rocking the boat by mentioning the past. If I'd known what I know now. . .'

She finished the sentence for him. 'We would have saved ourselves a lot of heartache.'

Alejandro nodded. 'I entirely agree.'

'And do you believe me now that I love you?'

'*Dios*, Tanya, I need my head examining for ever disbelieving you.' He drew her to him and kissed her. '*Mi corazón*, I promise I will never doubt anything you say to me again.'

'Alejandro, can I tell you that I think you are wonderful?'

He smiled. 'You are pretty fantastic yourself.'

'I don't mean that,' she said, knowing he was referring to the night they had spent together. 'I was thinking about the way you've brought Manolo up as your own. Not many men would do that. I've misjudged you. I thought you were a selfish womaniser. I thought you were stringing me along when it was really Juanita you loved. And I thought you were playing me off against Inocente. I didn't think you were capable of loving one woman alone.'

'Tanya, Tanya.' He cupped her face between his hands. 'There has never been anyone else for me but you. You were my first lover, and you will be my last. We will forget all the years between. I love you, Manolo loves you, and you love us. What more could a man ask for — except perhaps children of our own?'

Tanya nodded. 'I would like that too.'

'Will you marry me, Tanya?'

'Yes, Alejandro.'

'You will be happy living here?'

'Blissfully so.'

'We will get married on March the twenty-eighth, my saint's day.'

Tanya frowned. 'Your saint's day? What do you mean?'

He smiled. 'Every single day is a saint's day, and when it is your namesake then you celebrate also. It is a much bigger occasion than even your own birthday. So why not make it our wedding-day? You have three weeks to prepare yourself. Will that be enough?'

'More than enough. I'd readily marry you tomorrow.'

'And do my family out of all the excitement? I don't think we dare.' He kissed her again, and it was many minutes later when he said, 'Manolo will be growing impatient. Let us go and tell him that he is going to get a new *mamá*.'

Welcome to Europe

TENERIFE — 'the land of eternal spring'

Tenerife is quite simply a holiday paradise, combining all the comforts of home with touches of the exotic — such as the banana plantations you'll find. With its long beaches and sunny climate, and its relaxed, friendly atmosphere, it's the ideal destination for couples of all ages. Go to the top of Mount Teide, the highest mountain in Spain, or simply relax on the beach with a cool drink. . . The choice is yours.

THE ROMANTIC PAST

There is much debate about the history of the Canary Islands — how they came into being, where their early inhabitants came from, and how they got their name. Contrary to what you might think, the name seems to have nothing to do with canaries! Apparently there was an expedition to the islands in 30 BC, and large dogs were seen roaming around. As the Latin word for dog is *canis*, the lands became known as the Canis Islands.

The Spaniards arrived in the fifteenth century and found that the islands were inhabited by a primitive people known as the **Guanches**, who had blond hair and blue eyes, lived in caves and dressed in animal hide.

The Spanish started their conquest of the Canary Islands in 1402. This expedition was led by Béthencourt, who was so happy when he first saw the islands that he named the first two he came across Alegranza (Joy) and Graciosa (the Beautiful). Tenerife was the last of the islands to be conquered, falling to the Spanish in 1494, despite brave resistance by the Guanches.

A famous name associated with the Canary Islands is **Christopher Columbus**. Columbus might not actually have stayed on Tenerife, but his log book reveals that while he was sailing past it he saw an eruption of Mount Teide. . .which might explain why he didn't decide to stop there! However, he did stay on two of the other Canary Islands — on Gran Canaria and on Gomera, where it is rumoured that he had a love-affair with Beatriz de Bobadilla. Perhaps this is why he returned to the small island of Gomera on two further voyages!

Nelson probably had less pleasant memories of the Canary Islands. . . He lost an arm in Tenerife during the unsuccessful British attempt to conquer the islands in 1797.

THE ROMANTIC PRESENT — pastimes for lovers. . .

If you're going to Tenerife to enjoy a beach holiday you'll probably head for the south of the island, to a resort like **Playa de las Americas** or **Los Cristianos**. Of the two, Los Cristianos, which used to be a fishing village, is quieter and probably more attractive, with

Mount Teide making a spectacular backdrop. The large beach is an ideal place to sunbathe and relax with your partner.

There's no shortage of things to do in the evenings — Los Cristianos is well supplied with bars and restaurants, including many to make you feel you're 'home from home' with names like the British Bar and menus offering you English breakfasts and fish and chips. But if you want to try more typical Canarian cuisine, try exploring some of the back streets.

If you prefer smaller, less crowded beaches than those in Los Cristianos, try visiting **Abades**, on the south-east coast of the island, or Poris, which is just slightly further up.

If you want to do more than just lie on a beach, there are plenty of other parts of Tenerife just waiting to be explored. The capital of the island is **Santa Cruz**, where nearly a third of the island's population live. If you enjoy shopping, that alone is a good enough reason for a visit here — the shopping facilities are the best in Tenerife, with both small shops and larger stores with better quality goods. Start at the **Plaza de España**, and shop until you drop. . .

And if you're exhausted after that, why not visit the beautiful **Parque Municipal García Sanabria**? Wandering along its shady paths and admiring the sub-tropical plants and water gardens is guaranteed to relax you. Don't miss the well known floral clock at the entrance, or the impressive fountain at the centre.

If you're visiting the north of the island, you may well decide to stay in **Puerto de la Cruz**, the longest-established tourist resort and one which has its own distinctive character, with traditional old houses, cobbled roads and a seafront promenade.

Puerto de la Cruz and the surrounding area offer lots of activities. Visit the **Bananera El Guanche**, where you can learn all about how the banana grows and enjoy a banana and a taste of banana liqueur at the end of your tour. Don't miss a visit to the **Botanical Gardens**, where the exotic plants and trees include cinnamon trees, coffee plants and a rubber tree which is almost two hundred years old. Another interesting place to visit is **Loro Parque**. *Loro* is the Spanish word for parrot, and you will see parrots everywhere here. Some of them have even been trained to roller skate and ride tricycles!

Wherever you are on Tenerife, you can't fail to miss the majestic height of **Mount Teide**. A visit here is bound to be one of the highlights of your trip. You can take a cable car ride to just below the summit and, once there, enjoy a *lumumba* — a brandy-laced chocolate drink. If you're feeling active, it will take you about three quarters of an hour to walk to the summit from here, where you can admire the spectacular views.

If you want to discover 'traditional' Tenerife, rather than the places where all the tourists go, visit the tiny rustic villages of **La Sobrera** and **La Zarza** in the east of the island.

Or if history fascinates you, visit **Masca** in the northwest of the island. It is inland and set away from the road, and legend has it that it was discovered by a fisherman who was marooned on the beach at the foot of the valley. Walking inland, he came across this attractive area, went back to collect his family, and founded Masca. Today it is a tranquil, serene place with interesting architecture and narrow streets.

Try to make time to see the famous dragon tree — **El Drago** — in the north-west of the island. The tree is apparently over 3,000 years old. If it is cut it bleeds a red sap, or 'dragon's blood', which is how it got its name.

Whether you've spent the day exploring or sunning yourself, the evening is a time to go out and eat. Try a Canarian soup for a starter. **Sopa de berros** — watercress soup with herbs — is particularly recommended. Fish is usually good — why not try **cazuela canaria**, fish stew? To accompany your main meal, you might like to try a local dish called **papas arrugadas**. The literal translation of this — wrinkled potatoes — might not sound too appetising, but they're actually new potatoes cooked in their skin in well salted water, usually served with mojo sauce, made of oil, vinegar and local herbs.

And to drink, you can enjoy beer or wine. It's worth trying the well known **malvasia** and **moscatel** wines. You might also like to try **cobana** — a banana liqueur — and the local rum, called **ron**, which is sold everywhere and is quite strong! And if you don't feel like alcohol, the local mineral water is said to be excellent.

It's the end of your holiday, and after your stay here you're likely to have trouble packing all the **souvenirs** you've acquired into your suitcase! Choose from **hemstitch embroidery** — calados — which you might see local craftsmen at work on, **basketwork** — including palm-leaf baskets — and the **banana liqueur**, cobana. And if you really can't squeeze everything into your luggage, why not do as so many visitors have done. . .and return as soon as you can?

DID YOU KNOW THAT. . .?

*   Tenerife is the largest of the Canary Islands.

* Mount Teide in Tenerife is the **highest mountain** in Spain.

* you can throw **snowballs** on Mount Teide while people **sunbathe** twenty miles away.

* the unit of currency in Tenerife is the **peseta**.

* if you want to say 'I love you' when you're in Tenerife you can whisper *'Te quiero'*.

LOOK FOR OUR FOUR FABULOUS MEN!

Each month some of today's bestselling authors bring
four new fabulous men to Harlequin American Romance.
Whether they're rebel ranchers, millionaire power brokers
or sexy single dads, they're all gallant princes—and
they're all ready to sweep you into lighthearted fantasies
and contemporary fairy tales where anything is possible
and where all your dreams come true!

You don't even have to make a wish...Harlequin American
Romance will grant your every desire!

Look for Harlequin American Romance wherever Harlequin
books are sold!

HE SAID

♥

SHE SAID

Explore the mystery of male/female communication in this extraordinary new book from two of your favorite Harlequin authors.

Jasmine Cresswell and Margaret St. George bring you the exciting story of two romantic adversaries—each from their own point of view!

DEV'S STORY. CATHY'S STORY.
As he sees it. As she sees it.
Both sides of the story!

The heat is definitely on, and these two can't stay out of the kitchen!

Don't miss HE SAID, SHE SAID.
Available in July wherever Harlequin books are sold.

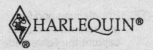

HARLEQUIN®

 **HARLEQUIN®**

Not The Same Old Story!

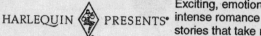 Exciting, emotionally
intense romance
stories that take readers
around the world.

 Vibrant stories of
captivating women
and irresistible men
experiencing the magic
of falling in love!

 Bold and adventurous—
Temptation is strong women,
bad boys, great sex!

 Provocative, passionate,
contemporary stories that
celebrate life and love.

 Romantic adventure
where anything is
possible and where
dreams come true.

 Heart-stopping, suspenseful
adventures that combine the
best of romance and mystery.

LOVE & LAUGHTER™ Entertaining and fun, humorous
and romantic—stories that
capture the lighter side of love.

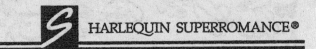

HARLEQUIN SUPERROMANCE®

...there's more to the story!

Superromance. A *big* satisfying read about unforgettable
characters. Each month we offer *four* very different
stories that range from family drama to adventure and
mystery, from highly emotional stories to romantic
comedies—and much more! Stories about people
you'll believe in and care about. Stories too
compelling to put down....

Our authors are among today's *best* romance writers.
You'll find familiar names and talented newcomers.
Many of them are award winners—and you'll see why!

If you want the biggest and best in romance fiction,
you'll get it from Superromance!
Available wherever Harlequin books are sold.

Look us up on-line at: http://www.romance.net

HS-GEN

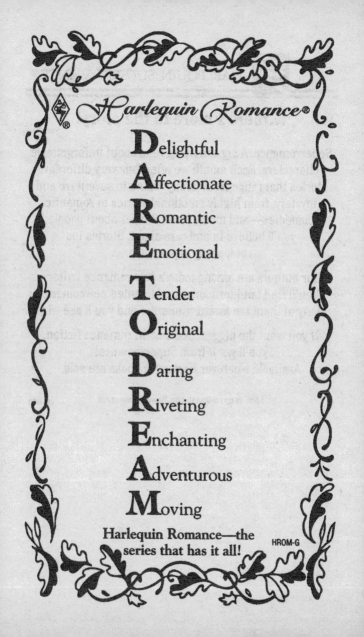

Harlequin Romance®

Delightful

Affectionate

Romantic

Emotional

Tender

Original

Daring

Riveting

Enchanting

Adventurous

Moving

Harlequin Romance—the
series that has it all!

HROM-G

HARLEQUIN ⬥ PRESENTS®

HARLEQUIN PRESENTS
men you won't be able to resist falling in love with...

HARLEQUIN PRESENTS
women who have feelings just like your own...

HARLEQUIN PRESENTS
powerful passion in exotic international settings...

HARLEQUIN PRESENTS
intense, dramatic stories that will keep you turning
to the very last page...

HARLEQUIN PRESENTS
The world's bestselling romance series!

Harlequin® Historical

If you're a serious fan of historical romance,
then you're in luck!

Harlequin Historicals brings you
stories by bestselling authors, rising new stars
and talented first-timers.

Ruth Langan & Theresa Michaels
Mary McBride & Cheryl St.John
Margaret Moore & Merline Lovelace
Julie Tetel & Nina Beaumont
Susan Amarillas & Ana Seymour
Deborah Simmons & Linda Castle
Cassandra Austin & Emily French
Miranda Jarrett & Suzanne Barclay
DeLoras Scott & Laurie Grant...

You'll never run out of favorites.

Harlequin Historicals...they're too good to miss!

HH-GEN